The Wheel Keeper

The Wheel Keeper

ROBERT PEPPER-SMITH

National Library of Canada Cataloguing in Publication Data
Pepper-Smith, Robert, 1954-
The wheel keeper

(Nunatak fiction)
ISBN 1-896300-49-9

I. Title. II. Series.
PS8581.E634W43 2002   C813'.6   C2002-910983-3
PR9199.4.P46W43 2002

Editor for the Press: Thomas Wharton
Cover and interior design: Ruth Linka
Author photo: Kit Pepper

NeWest Press acknowledges the support of the Canada Council for the Arts, the Alberta Foundation for the Arts, and the Edmonton Arts Council for our publishing program. We also acknowledge the financial support of the Government of Canada through the Book Publishing Industry Development Program (BPIDP) for our publishing activities.

NeWest Press
201–8540–109 Street
Edmonton, Alberta T6G 1E6
(780) 432-9427
www.newestpress.com

02   03   04   05   4   3   2   1

PRINTED AND BOUND IN CANADA

This story is dedicated to the memory of
Lucy Guzzo
Dolores Guzzo
Tom Smith

From the late 1800s on, many left Roca D'Avola in southern Italy to work the orchards and vineyards of the Argentine and British Columbia. Every season they would go and many would return. They were called the *golondrinas* : the swallows. Often, with false papers or with an illegitimate child, they saw their way under the eyes of the authorities by cunning, disguise, and quick flight. They learned the illusion of promises: a 1908 brochure advertising land grants and work on the Canadian railroad flaps on the mayoralty walls and on the door of Tommassini's café in the Roca piazza. It shows a verdant valley, a river called the Illecillewaet. When you examine the brochure photo closely, you see a forest of black and grey spires, the green and blue fronds painted on.

Often, survival for the golondrinas depended on a recognizable sign: boots made by Giacometti on the Via dei Mutaliti, a yellow accordion, a word, or an accent carried under your tongue. We offer this *signe* to our children, to make it easy to see where we're from.

The Italian-Canadian Association of R.

*D*riving over the rise of the new highway, I see below me the long grey reservoir that was once the K. valley. Wet flakes scatter from the cloud cover that has settled between the mountains, and a wind—leaping like a cat—raises a steely shimmer near the shore, then farther out. Except for the wind in the spruce and firs, and in the abandoned orchards above the takeline, there is no sound on the reservoir, and I recall with a shock that as a child of five I saw this grey mass long before it was. I recognized it and I felt that it recognized me.

Below the surface of the lake is the village where I was born and lived till I was fifteen. I stand on the shoreline and try to trace by the mountain peaks and by the avalanche tracks how it once was: the village of ninety houses stood there on a far riverbank. In the village, the house my family shared with nostre nonna was called "the castle" because it was built out of Italian stone to last. Now its hallways are currents, with the fish we call redfish in them. Before the dam chutes were closed for the first time, before the water crept into the felled orchards and torn-up vineyards, many of the village houses were burned and plowed into their cellars or moved to a new site above the takeline. That site was soon abandoned because of the dust storms that rose from the reservoir bed when vast amounts of water were let down during the summer to feed American dams. A railway bridge with a cedar catwalk under it crossed the river from the village to this hillside. It too was dismantled. It crossed below me where I now stand, and below me stood the Pradolini house where my aunt Manice and my cousin Anna lived briefly. The Pradolini house where the golondrinas used to stay during the harvest.

I

In our family a story is told of a child who went through the wheel of Roca D'Avola and was returned into the arms of her mother.

Many infants who went through the wheels of southern Italy died within a year.

So it was remarkable that Manice lived.

And only because of the help of the wheel keeper—a Scottish slater of eighteen, my grandfather.

Children vanish. They vanish through doors, under stairs, in the branches of apricot trees. They can be seen on the railroad bridge, on a catwalk of wooden planks, the river far below.

In a dream I have my mother rises from her bed, floats away. I grip her by the ankle to pull her down. In another dream my father is absorbed into the alcove wall of our apartment on the street of the grandmothers. The wall takes him in like water.

The night my cousin Anna—ill with appendicitis—was brought by ferry across the river, I was standing on nostre nonna's porch roof. Anna was my aunt Manice's daughter. I'd parted our kitchen curtains to climb out. I could smell smoke from across the river. Less used, the doors. You take a heap of stone and planks, you put it together and you have a house.

> *What is a house that goes as far as a breath?*
> *It's for human beings to live in, Anna.*

I had heard the village cars and trucks first in the street of the grandmothers and then farther away, quiet in the way they came together on the potholed road that led south of our village. Asleep, I was dreaming of the way Our Lady of Sorrows rings to announce an avalanche or a fire and when I awoke the bell's ringing became the low idle of the village engines, first in our street, then farther away. Cars and tractors were coming in from the vineyards onto the road to light up the runway on the southern flats.

Wait, my uncle would say, that's how he would announce a riddle for which he'd immediately supply the answer.

Why is our road full of potholes?

Nests for the fishes!

I'd climbed through the kitchen window onto the porch roof to watch the long string of headlamps, the bright glare of the aircraft lights on the tractor my uncle used to hunt night deer in his vineyard on the Georgia

Bench. I heard a rustling in the chestnut tree by the porch.

The train station was lit up and behind it the shadow of the mountain, the glaciers above the treeline. Long gashes in the mountain forest, the tracks of avalanches. And in our garden by the cedar fence, the madonna's cart in grape leaves and ribbons, the odour of dill torches.

This house had been built by Albert Murray, my grandfather, over forty years ago. In the village it was called "the castle" because it was the only house built of stone with two kitchens, the summer one downstairs, the winter one upstairs with its iron stove. The year Anna was born we moved into the castle's upstairs apartment. After months of no work, my father had gotten the job as captain of the river ferry. He was also the deckhand and the ticket collector. To signal that you wanted to cross you rang a bell. There was room for three cars to be taken to the road on the other side of the river, the road that went south into the valley orchards and vineyards. I remember his first uniform: the grey pants with the long black stripe, the blue jacket with provincial crests for shoulder patches, the grey cap with a peaked visor.

Those who know the river, he said to my mother. Those who know the river!

He was standing in the doorway, wearing the same smile as when he brought home a redfish or, one fall, a pair of deer antlers and a bloody skullcap—food on the table.

On the porch roof, I saw fires across the river near the railroad bridge: the Pradolini house and the Swede's barn. The drone of an airplane shimmered above the fire, the house turned to breath. I felt like running to warn the grown-ups. I can still feel panic fluttering in my stomach at the memory of those fires, always at night, always on a warm night when the air was still.

Wait, my uncle would say. How does the Hydro take the heart out of us?

They burn our neighbour's house. Their machines trample fences.

A little grape syrup in their tanks, he suggested, to stop them.

The night the call came for Anna, my father, getting out of bed to answer it, touched my ankle. I was asleep in the cot by the big stove we called the iron monster. As black as a locomotive, it darkened half the kitchen wall.

Anna's not well, my father said. I have to bring her across the river.

In the foyer at the top of the stairs that led down to the first floor he was putting on his ferryman's jacket and cloth cap.

My mother who was with him said, We'll be back soon.

I felt then that they wouldn't be back soon. How can you count on such hurried promises? When Anna was born ten years previous to that night she was not expected to live. I was told that, born prematurely, she was kept in a shoebox on my aunt Manice's stove. I don't remember the shoebox. I do remember my fear that she would vanish, though I felt responsible for protecting her. She lacked the bones that would weigh her to earth.

I was also told, She will be like a sister to you. I understood that to mean: carry her like the madonna under your coat, or like a bird in your hands. And yet I who was to protect her had been left behind.

II

In our family the *ruotaro*, the wheel keeper, was used to threaten us. He was said to ride a horse with wicker saddlebaskets for *l'innocenti*. His infants came from the Roca D'Avola *ospizia*. In wicker baskets he took them to the ospizia in Napoli. Some died on the way. *Innocenti, esposito*: children of the wheel. In my dreams he's a small, slight man with willowy ankles who rides a plowhorse. I was told that he always left for Napoli after dark—that you could hear the hollow clop of horse's hooves in the Roca D'Avola streets and, if you listened, cries muffled by the baskets.

Once, climbing into an apricot tree in nostre nonna's garden, I broke a main branch. She chased me with a cedar stake used to hold up a vine. From the swaying young tree I'd watch her walk among the high vines in her backyard garden to a barrow. She picked a few peas, shelled and chewed them to a paste. She uprooted a few of the dying stalks and laid them across the path. As she moved the barrow to the end of the row, the wheel shrieked. She opened the faucet near the coal chute and a plume of sprinkler water swept across the pea vines toward the apricot tree. To avoid the water I climbed out on a branch to lower myself to the ground. It snapped and she heard it.

Beyond the backyard gate rose the stucco wall of the Community Centre. A blind wall on that side, with a rickety flight that climbed to the one fire door, high up.

I hid there.

She called for me and I hid behind the railing, laughing behind the wooden slats.

Come down, she shouted. Or I'll send the ruotaro for you.

That was the summer of 195_. I was five years old.

A week later, the St. Leon hospital called to say that my aunt Manice was about to have a baby. There are complications, the nurse said over the telephone. We—my father, nostre nonna and I—took the south road through the orchards on the other side of the river. The gravel road led through cherry and peach orchards and there were tall, grey-boned ladders in the peach trees. Though it was dusk, through the car window I could see the pickers on the ladders and at the roadside bins, emptying the fruit into them. The cloth sacks they carried were round and full. A strong odour of ripe peaches came through the back seat window that I'd opened. The pickers wore long-sleeved shirts and blouses to protect themselves from the peach skins; I could see them in the trees at dusk on the ladders, the white shirts and blouses among the masses of dusty leaves. Ten or twelve, but there always seemed to be many more. That feeling came from their voices, from the languages I couldn't understand welling through the leaves. Portuguese, Italian, high up in the trees on the grey-boned ladders. I remember the smells and how they carried the ladders slung on a shoulder, golondrinas flown in for the harvest. The white shirts were coming out of the orchards then toward the road, going to tables under lanterns hung in the trees. Women at the tables were canning the fruit too ripe to sell.

The car was raising dust billows behind it, gravel rattling on the floor panels. We had taken the gravel road because of the call from the hospital and my father was driving the same way he piloted the river ferry—with the intent, searching look of one who watches below surfaces.

We went over the crest and below was the river, much wider here. I had never seen such water before. Though it lay far away between the hills, it seemed to fill the windshield with its own soft light. The sudden smell of winds reminded me of melting snowfields above the village. We were going down the St. Leon road toward the river. The tug toward the mass of grey water was so strong that I knew we would not live. Because of my fear I no longer heard the gravel that was rattling against the floor panels. The hurry was Anna's birth; nostre nonna, sitting by my father, urged him on. Watching the roadside for deer, he was not paying attention to the turn in the road.

I had to put down an anchor. I slipped off a dress shoe that smelled of nostre nonna's cellar where it had been stored on a shelf above the floodline, maybe for years. Nostre nonna had placed it in my hands for Anna's birth. I balanced the shoe in the open car window, then pushed it out.

By the time my father understood what had happened, we were a mile down the road.

Without saying anything he pulled over, got out of the car and walked away alone. His bowed shoulders and stiff walk said, You can't show up for your cousin's birth in one shoe!

Nostre nonna sat in the passenger seat without turning around. She wore a kerchief and beads of sweat had gathered on her neck. "*Bambino piccola*, we won't be there on time."

High branches over the trampled grass beneath the trees, three-legged ladders propped against the trunks. By then it was dark; nostre nonna had spread the dress she'd brought from the car in the grass, for me to lie down on.

Go to sleep, she said.

The canning fires lit up the pots hung over them and the trunks. I could see gleaming knives as the women worked. A woman with a long ponytail brought us some food from a table. Later I'd learn to call her the Calabrianne.

Boy, she smiled. Where is your shoe?

I dropped it out the window.

Why did you drop your shoe out the window?

Grandmother said we were going to drown.

Nonna looked at me out of her astonished eyes.

That we were going to drown, I nodded.

She reached over to shake me.

I remember that the first time I saw my aunt Manice was in late summer of the 195_ harvest, a few weeks before Anna was born. Because nostre nonna was ill that summer, she had crossed the river to help with the harvest.

I was sent across the room to Manice.

Head bowed, she sat alone at the end of the breakfast table.

My father had placed something cold in my hand, folded over my fingers: "Take that to your aunt." It was a two-year-old piece of her wedding cake wrapped in tin-foil. It was his way of saying, I know your marriage is finished. Without opening it, Manice slid the foil package into a patch pocket on her loose, ash-grey dress that had four wooden buttons up the front of it.

Your aunt Manice. I stared at her, open-mouthed. Till then, I'd known nothing about her. Her dress was that of a poor fieldworker. Her black blouse was also very loose and had old-fashioned wooden buttons. She had a broad, gentle, almost shy face with clear brown eyes. Her hair was tied up in a kerchief, like a village grandmother's.

I went up to her. I pressed my hand on her belly.

After her hip operation nostre nonna said, I pinched myself to make sure I was awake. As the effects of the anaesthetic wore off, she wasn't sure whether she was dreaming or awake. Now I placed my five-year-old hand on Manice's belly, to make sure she was real.

You're my sister's son, she said. Your name is Michael Guzzo.

Yes, I nodded.

Do you know where I live?

I shook my head.

I live south of here on the St. Leon road. You should come to visit me. I have my own orchard where the dam is being built.

Caught by her clear brown eyes, I'd forgotten my hand on her rounded belly.

Kicks, I said. Like a rabbit.

Yes, she nodded, a rabbit. I'm going to have a baby who will be your cousin.

She told me she was married to my uncle Paolo, though I'd never seen them together. I had no idea that he was twice married and had two families, one at each end of the valley. To keep his secret he had forbidden Manice to visit us. Now everyone knew though nothing was said.

Manice and Paolo sat at opposite ends of the table and did not look at each other. Or they looked through each other and spoke as if the other were not there. My uncle spoke loudly and cheerfully. He had seen my father return the wrapped piece of wedding cake to Manice and from that moment on his voice was loud.

I knew several of the golondrinas at the breakfast table, but Manice I did not know, and I kept my eyes on her. She didn't say anything. She ate little and put down the knife and then the fork with its tines on the plate rim.

In those days of light dew we began early and picked till midday. To lift the dew, my uncle Paolo, who had raised a glass, said, We are people for this harvest; we are people for seven harvests from now! We all knew this Aconcagua saying of his that broke in during the meal. He was from the Aconcagua in the Argentine. His family had worked the vineyards there, and when he was twelve they emigrated to Canada. My uncle worked on the trains. He'd been a trainman most of his life, a fireman shovelling coal till he became an engineer. Paolo I'd see almost every day, and at night I'd hear his engine that we called the Sentinella. From every train came the long whistle followed by a short blast. But each was as individual as a voice, and from as early as I can remember I'd learned to identify the Sentinella's whistle on the mountain, our sleep, the dark village. Now it was whispered that he had another family in Field and that the girl who sat beside him—the girl who had arrived in the cab of the Sentinella—was his daughter Maren from there.

Maren is with me, he told me, leaning across the table.

I was hiding the fried egg I didn't like under the rim of my plate. When I saw that Manice was watching me, I slid under the table to crawl away. The tablecloth hung down on both sides, making a kind of tent with legs and boots tucked under the walls. The new cousin had slid down beside me.

What's your name?

Maren Pradolini, she said. She had green eyes and a slender chin.

Long neck, she called me. Like a horse.

My uncle caught me between his boots. He lifted me to touch the rosette of sculpted fruit and birds around the ceiling light. "Is it damp?" A damp rosette meant wasps in the vineyard.

No, I said. I looked out of his strong hands at that girl who had crawled into the chair beside his. Slender chin, green eyes, a mocking smile.

He was telling the girl about Bennello's new plane. On the side my uncle sold dynamite to mines in the mountains, and he and Bennello flew it in.

We'll take you up tomorrow, he promised her. Then I heard him whisper, Go to your nonna, sit by her. She's rich in vineyards and houses. She doesn't know you well yet.

Wait till the dew has lifted. After the breakfast, we stood at the vineyard gate by iron scales used to weigh grape bins. The pickers had brought the wooden bins on high-wheeled carts. The fence posts were already warm and the dew had gone from the wire fence. Some of the pickers had strings looped in their belts to tie the legs of netted birds for their soup.

Smell the sugar! my uncle shouted.

Empty bins scrubbed with sulphur water at the gate— the first morning of the harvest. Men and women from Italy and Portugal wore rubber gloves against the wasps.

Do you hear?

When I nodded, my uncle smiled.

He opened the gate and to safeguard our luck, I darted among the vines. As soon as they heard the clatter of stones under my feet, the birds struggled.

Caught wing and neck, one tried to fly through the nets over the ripe grapes.

The bird weighed nothing and it throbbed like a bell. I covered its eyes to pretend night. Yet it's our smell that overpowers them. I was still young, without the odour of the soup-makers. Freed wing, the gaping beak. I cupped it for a moment, the throbbing bell of damp feathers, then tossed it over the vines.

A few weeks later, because of the call from the hospital we were going to Manice's house. The car parked on the shoulder of the St. Leon road, I was unable to sleep on the dress that my grandmother had spread in the grass by the canning fires. I remember feeling that days had passed, though my father had hardly been gone an hour for the shoe. To avoid nonna's anxious, impatient eyes I hid under a smokey blanket that the Calabrianne had brought.

When my father returned with the pushed-out shoe,

he threatened, If you throw it out the window again, you'll walk for it!

Nonna had fallen asleep in the front seat. As we drove south along the river, I could hear her head knocking against the door window. I wanted to wake her up: such sleep was reckless, too trusting. I didn't know what she was dreaming, why her head knocked against the window like a doll's.

We turned into a lane that led through Manice's orchards to a house that was dark, silent. It was one of those small wooden houses built during the war, so strong that Manice had had it moved here from St. Leon and put on a stone foundation. Behind the bedroom curtain that my father drew aside stood a high brass bed with a carved headboard. Nostre nonna opened the window that looked out over the orchards and the road lined with canning fires. I watched the three or four wasps chewing on the sash outside the flyscreen while my father lifted my suitcase onto the bed.

What have you brought? he joked. What have you got in there, bones? You plan to stay forever.

Nostre nonna took my hand. I buried my face in her midriff that smelled of oranges placed to dry under the stove. Manice was in the St. Leon hospital.

I slept in Manice's bed with nostre nonna. Anna was born that night. I awoke to my father's voice returned from the hospital, his words turning over in the darkened room. Through the still window curtains I could see the dark shapes of the trees. The warm night air smelled of dry grass and smoke. I heard a truck passing on the gravel road. The darkness weighed like a breath on my cheek. There was a dull gleam on the sash, where the wasps had fed.

The murmuring of two voices. Yes they were speaking, but I hardly heard anything: the words breathed in and out, distant and strong, voices that enter and leave and just before you fall asleep echo in a tin pot.

While she and my father talked, nostre nonna gripped my ankle. I felt that without gripping my ankle she would have drifted from the bed, from the sheets, from the warmth of the canning fires that burned all night. Her hand was cold; she was warming her fingers where her skin touched mine. My blood fled to warm hers, and at the same time the soft murmur of the voices fell around me, to the sheets, on my lips and eyelashes.

The heart has a peculiar past; everything that has affected it is present to it. My grandmother was telling my father how she had once climbed through the orchards of Roca D'Avola in Italy with her first child in her arms. Around the baby's neck she had tied with a red silk string a picture of a saint torn from a calender, the *segni di riconoscimento*. Before she could marry the baby's father, he had died on the road to Napoli. He was taking baskets of fruit and nuts to the Napoli markets and, drunk, he'd fallen from his horse. "Unmarried, I must *make the gesture* of giving up the child."

The ospizia she was climbing towards had a wooden box that rotated in the wall facing the village. She placed the infant in the box, which was called the *rouota*–the wheel. To awaken the wheel keeper, she tugged on the bellcord. A clear night: above, a swath of stars, a high warm wind booming through the trees. She touched the rolled picture of the saint, the two closed eyelids. "Then I turned the box into the wall."

By signs of recognition we say, We'll come back for

you; we'll bring you home soon. The shred of cloth, the piece of ribbon, a picture torn from a calender—all catalogued, preserved. Images of saints, foreign coins, torn pieces of coloured cloth: segni di riconoscimento, signs of recognition. That night, the ruotaro takes the baby into the village. The mayor examines l'innocenti, checks her sex. She is healthy, well-fed. He opens the registry.

He asks the wheel keeper if the mother has made the required payment.

I never saw her, he replies.

What name have you given her?

Manice Esposito.

The village mayor checks the registry, running his thumb down the entries.

The next morning nostre nonna is at the ospizia gate posing as a wet nurse. "The mayor of Roca D'Avola has sent me to nurse l'innocenti."

The wheel keeper—a young boy of eighteen, our grandfather—looked at her, laughed.

You're the mother, he said.

I am the wet nurse hired by the mayor.

No, you are the mother who pretends to be a wet nurse.

How do you know?

By the smell of your milk, he says lightly.

The blood trusts, I heard nonna say to my father, still I carried a knife. He led me to my child.

Here is Manice Esposito, he said.

Then it was my turn to laugh. Who says Manice Esposito—who gave her that name?

I did, said the ruotaro.

It was already written in the wheel keeper's book:

Manice Esposito, born August 11, 1920 with
a picture of San Giovanni Neponani tied
around her neck with a red silk string.

The day nostre nonna brought Anna home, I was helping
my father fork up potatoes in Manice's garden.

Who is getting born? I asked.

Your cousin is getting born. My father laughed,
straightening his back.

Your cousin is born, he said, but you say she is getting born.

How long does that take?

He looked at me out of his amused eyes. His eyes
were shaped like those of a sparrow and they had the
same dark colour.

You and she will be friends, he said.

I was required to hold Anna.

I was made to sit on the porch steps while nostre
nonna got out of the car. She crossed the yard to place
the bundle in my lap. I remember feeling that they'd
wrapped cousin Anna to hold her together. Only the
screwed-up face showed through the swaddled cloth. A
face with scratches on it, pale blue eyes, a fringe of thick
dark hair.

You will be friends, nonna said. She will be like a sister to you.

Anna weighed almost nothing in my lap and I felt
like pushing her off. I was instructed not to free her arms,
not to untie the mitts from her hands, "because she could
scratch her face."

That Fall I hunted in the orchards and in the outbuildings for bones. Something to hold you together, was the feeling I had. I didn't want to see a lot of Anna, only I was afraid that once out of my sight she would be taken away somewhere. "You and she will be friends. She will be like a sister to you." Then began my mistrust of words, of pronouncements. To make the cousin whole I hunted for bones: pellets from an owl's stomach, a heap of burst calf skulls by the roadside, the hawk skull on a shelf in the barn.

That child slept in a shoebox. There was goat's milk with her, an eyedropper. Her legs were no longer than a man's finger. How those stories get told in families, with laughter: "No longer than your finger," "in a shoebox kept on the stove," "not expected to live," "by the smell of your milk."

We called you "the baby" till Manice returned from the hospital with a name for you.

I followed nostre nonna up the flight to Anna's bedroom. Nostre nonna had found the path with the fewest creaks; I remember her milky, carefully placed ankles, the way her hand glided along the banister. With twigs and a wood chip my father had demonstrated how they rolled this house, lifted from its foundations, on logs across the tracks in St. Leon. It seemed strange that it could have been moved here, many miles away. When nostre nonna's cellar flooded, I felt that her house would float away, that one morning I'd find only water lapping the cellar walls.

Nostre nonna showed me Anna in her crib. Slept in a shoebox people say, not expected to live. But I remember that even then she was too big for a shoebox and that her eyes were open to look at us when we came in. Only her head and face peered out of the blanket that she was wrapped in. She sucked milk from an eyedropper while I held the dish with the goat's milk in it. She never seemed to sleep. She was always wide awake with those wide eyes, now grey, now slate blue, and I tried to get her to look at me: I rapped softly on the crib railing. Her hand like a wrinkled water flower: touch the palm and it closes, draw out your finger and it opens. To make her whole, I placed the sack of bones under the crib.

Paolo called the next morning.

How's the bambina piccola? Does she have all her toes and fingers? What's her name? I remember that the forced cheeriness of his rapid-fire questions astonished me. "You tell the grandmother I'll be down soon. In the Sentinella!"

For three or four nights in a row I listened for the Sentinella's whistle on the tracks by the river. Once I heard the clatter of hooves in the gravel outside the house and I imagined that the ruotaro had climbed through the cousin's window to place her in a wicker basket among others. In my fear I sat up in bed to listen for the cry of the basketed little ones. I realized the cousin had no name and nothing tied to her, *nothing to say she was ours.*

A week after my aunt Manice had returned from the hospital, I was riding the bicycle that nostre nonna had bought for my cousin Anna, just born. The lane climbed through Manice's orchards, and I was on the crest. Below was the river, placid that morning, a glittering ribbon that reflected the hills on the far shore. The bike rocked as it went downhill. Nostre nonna had raised the training wheels with a wrench from her pocket. Soon I was going faster than I'd ever gone before. The wind rushed into my mouth, drying it. I crossed the river road at the foot of the orchard and flew over a stone embankment.

Nostre nonna found me in a heap under the bicycle. She took me to the same hospital in St. Leon where Anna was born. That hospital is now underwater, the hallways currents, the fish we call redfish in them. She stood at the foot of my bed. She cowled her head with her kerchief, so that only her eyes showed through.

Nonna, what do you want?

I am the ruotaro, she said, changing her voice into a man's that made me laugh. I've come to take all the little boys who are never home for supper.

She made the sound of hoof beats on the painted radiator under the window, rapping it with her palms.

No, I remember saying to her. It's the cousin you want.

III

Birds feel the death in our hands. As a young girl nostre nonna was the bird-freer in the vineyards of Roca D'Avola. These vineyards were below the padrone's pine forest, and they had the rare stock dove and the skylark in them. Before the harvest could begin she would go among the netted vines to free entangled birds. Otherwise they'd make the pickers' soup, which the padrone considered to be very, very bad luck for the harvest. Nostre nonna freed them without harm; she had delicate, patient fingers, yet there was no physical reason for her success. In her hands a bird stilled while she covered its eyes with her palm.

She would cover our grandfather's eyes with her hands to make him sleep. Her success, he said, had more to do with the smell of her calloused hands than with their warmth. Your hands smell like stone, he told her once, Anjou stone.

The story begins in 1920. My grandfather is riding a bicycle from Dundee, Scotland through France to Italy. His father was a master slater in Dundee, his mother a weaver. I see him pedalling south to Italy on a bicycle with low-slung handlebars. In the bag strapped over the rear fender he carries a slater's hammer and a coil of copper wire. He is going south from the twenty-four-hour jute factories of Dundee, where there is no work for young men, to the village where his father had once cut and packed slate for the roof of the Lelands courthouse, a pale abalone-green slate to set off the dull brick of the building. His father and mother—my great grandparents—had met in the village near the Italian quarry; she was a sharecropper who worked in the orchards and vineyards of Roca D'Avola. When he left for Scotland with the slate packed in straw in crates, she accompanied him.

From his mother my grandfather had learned the dialect of the region; he was fluent in Italian. When he told her of his plans, she asked him to see to a debt that she'd left behind: a few lire owed to Tommassini, the owner of the trattoria in the piazza. After so many years that debt would have to be paid in a memorable fashion, perhaps with a goat.

Wet snow was falling in the streets of Roca D'Avola—an event for the village. He rode under snow that fell out of the heavy low sky and when he looked up the flakes themselves turned grey. In France, he'd stopped at a hillside inn of Anjou to notice the town roofs, patterns of metallic slate for the sun's reflection:

Comme les cheveux d'une jeune fille, said the innkeeper.

Where the *albero*—the festival pole—was usually planted outside the village church of Roca, a moon-tugged boulder had shouldered its way through the earth over winter, to lie hidden beneath the cobblestones. Men with pickaxes and shovels were digging a hole for l'albero. They'd uncovered a dun-coloured boulder that now wore a little cap of snow, impossible to go on.

We dug here last year, one of them muttered. And it was good digging, too.

Albert Murray heard the priest in the church doorway say *Festa paesane* in his little voice of disgust.

One among them turned to a young woman, very pregnant:

Lucia, bring us some water to drink from Tommassini's, in a voice that had the authority of a father.

Albert Murray leapt onto the back of the stone. He felt its back, a gentle brushing of the fingertips. He had such fine, strong hands at eighteen, grey stone dust under the fingernails. One nail, split, was bound with string tied in a knot.

Lucia, he said to the pregnant girl, a glass of Tommassini water.

This he poured into the fine cracks in the stone. He knelt down to listen, to feel for the exhaled air with his lips.

He knew in accepting the glass the trace of her elbow, of her lips, the trace of her voice like stone dust on a sill. Where are you from, she'd asked. You speak like us.

Dundee, he told her. All the way from Scotland. Hopped onto the back of the stone, he who had brought a goat to settle an old debt. The gentle tapping over the stone: here, he said, here and here. Listen to how the voice changes. That kind of talking takes awhile; it goes behind and underneath. And with a few quick blows the boulder is broken up.

The priest who had watched from the church doorway hired him to repair the ospizia's northern wall that had been damaged by a mudslide. He could tell this boy who spoke with the accent of the region knew how to work stone. Presently the ospizia housed no innocenti. They had been sent into the hills to wet nurses, their names in a book. And it was not a thick registry for a village.

Lucia was not used to it, thick about the shoulders, to bind the hair under the scarf, how to twist and curl the mass. She felt its weight as though it were not her own as she carried her child, only a few days old, through the orchards behind the village, to place her in the rouota: because she was unmarried, it was the demand of the priest. Her hair had grown long since her brother had left for Canada, and she'd left it uncut. Sky bright with stars, a booming wind in the trees. I'll cut it when I see you again, she'd told him.

That night Albert Murray was the ruotaro. Usually this task was given to the wet nurses of the ospizia, closed down now because of the damaged northern wall. He drove sheep out of the ospizia orchard with handfuls of snow. When the snow pelted one of the sheep, staining its coat, the animal would trot for a few feet and then stand gazing straight ahead with darkened eyes as if listening. He remembered the priest's instructions: Now that you're repairing the ospizia wall, he'd said, it is possible that a mother will use the wheel. Try to get a payment from her before she vanishes. If there is a signe attached to the infant, carefully record its details in the book of the wheelkeeper. Preserve the signe, no matter how tattered and worthless.

Before entering the ospizia, the slater rolled his long trousers above the bird-thin ankles, rolled the trousers so as to make no sound as he went down the corridor with its plaster walls, by rooms open to the hills. Much later that night, while he was reading by lamplight, he heard the creak of the turning wheel, then an infant's cry.

A week later she lay beside the slater to listen, as when you strain every nerve to hear a cry baffled by the wind. I describe him precisely as she described him to me: he disappeared into his hands. Asleep, he wrapped himself in his hands as in wood; the milk from her breasts wet his shoulders.

In the morning he sat at the empty table and he said, conjuring an imaginary breakfast with his fluttering hands, I myself generally have some porridge and milk, a little tea, a slice of bread and ham, and, as far as I can afford it, a little steak. For dinner I generally have broth; sometimes potatoes and milk; and I generally take tea at night, with bread and cheese, or bread and butter, with a slice of toast.

She smiled, shaking the slater's conjuring hands that placed the imaginary porridge and milk at the empty table as if to awaken him.

What is toast? She blew gently in his eyes. Full of smoke, she said, we have no toast here.

Where are you going? He had felt in the way she looked at him and in her smile her plans to leave.

Vlanmore in Canada, she told him. Or I'll lose my child to the priests.

Another time: Sanmore, the word a blur in her mouth, dream smudge. All the months of letters from her brother, then the invitation: the money order for passage. The extravagance of paper, printed land brochures with coloured reproductions of a painting that showed the Illecillewaet River with a boat on it, a mountain forest.

What does it say?

He looked at her.

I can't read, she said.

He traced out the words, blotting them: the cracked nail. "What's the stone like on this river the Canadians call the Illecillewaet?"

The stone?

Yes, he whispers in her ear. The slate.

For the infant Manice he gouged the skin of a North African plum, the pit a lump of yellow ice. He licked the juice from her belly and tossed her in the air. Manice Tomorrow, he said, Manice Tomorrow, see what tomorrow may bring, and he laughed, flashing his bright little teeth while he tottered around the room on his bird ankles, tossing the laughing child into the air with her plum-sticky belly. He tossed her up and up with her fat little arms spread and the fingers spread to grip the air. To you, he said. To your mother who is going to Sanmore, Vlanmore. And I am yours, yours in the big light of this place, with its big booming orchard winds.

See my teeth, he smiled. You have no teeth; all you have is a dirty chin, wiping her face with his shirt-tail.

We will play emigrants now.

The bed is our boat, or hide under the bed till your momma comes home.

The whole village smelled of oregano. She was out cutting oregano on the hills, to be brought to Napoli in sacks on horses. She spread it to dry under the eucalyptus trees. The money her brother had sent wasn't enough to cover passage to Montreal and a train ticket to the village beyond the Rockies called Sanmore or Vlanmore, where her brother had set up a bootmaker's shop. While Albert Murray repaired the ospizia wall and tended the child he'd named Manice, the child who was not his own, she cut oregano on the hills to make up the difference.

Her fingertips, glistening with oil, made tracks on the wall by the bed. The ospizia wall of rough plaster, in the hillside orchards.

Vine stalks blackened with philloxera among the trees.

From each room with its windows flung wide open came a wind carrying the earth odour of oregano. It walked her down a long corridor booming with wind by old plaster walls. She carried a sack of her clothes under her arm.

His breath was between a sigh and a whistle as he followed her down the corridor, and she always stayed with him till he slept.

Or sometimes till she slept.

Touch my lips she says to him and his touch is the air.

Touch me she says and his touch on her cheek is like a breeze. All of a sudden she is asleep, head on his chest. He takes in the track of fingerprints on the wall, and through the window the tall trees that border the ospizia, the various shadows that have laid open the orchard. He takes in the fluttering, the wild fluttering of ribbons tied to the tree marked for the l'albero. The wind that rushes to them is a good dry wind from the hillside: it smells of winter stones the size of oranges.

There is honour in local stone.

It honours the soil and the light and the moderating effects of the valley. It allows you to distinguish between what is foreign and what is kin to you. It makes you feel that you are growing from the inside outwards.

It's time, she said, rising to dress him.

Once a terrified bird flew through the window into her hair.

He was looking at her, laughing; he had seen it before she had. The laughter on his lips like a light froth; who knows how long he had lain there, watching her sleep.

She shook her lifted head, flaring her nostrils, remembering the smell of his hands on her face.

The baby, too, had touched her and she held its face near hers. She swaddled Manice and stroked her forehead till she slept, humming whatever came to mind, words that drifted in and out of meaning, and sometimes she would laugh low at what she heard herself sing:

> There are those who uproot and those who plant
> There are those who plant and those who uproot
> On the priests lightning and thunder
> Lightning and thunder upon the priests
> Not a hoe the sickle
> And the sickle is not a hoe

Not egg the lemon
The lemon is not an egg

How strange their night laughter sounds! The soft laughter of the low-lying ice mist that has crept into the orchards.

They remember: the cut-up olive and amandier branches, firewood stacked by the door.

I did that for you, she reminds him.

And their faces in the winter, so warm.

The shadows of her arms fall across the window slats as she measures the size of the moon with her fists, one atop the other. They can smell the low-lying mist that climbs on its knees into the lower orchard like a planting drunk, late at night, so late at night under such a moon that the earth lows and drifts, dark and dank. The three-fisted moon throws slats of light across her shoulders, her hair, and she listens for the priest's footsteps as she does every night, hardly able to sleep. She says, If he hears about us, he'll come for my child. To take her to the ospizia in Napoli.

I will dress you, I said to him. If I leave now I'll be noticed and caught.

No, I will do it.

No, I said. Don't you see? To fool the priest's eyes, you must be dressed in a woman's clothes with a woman's hands.

The next morning, in an oregano cart, Albert Murray leaves for Napoli with my child.

Segni di riconoscimento: in the ospizia the slater led me by the hand into a room of cluttered wooden shelves. It was like a shop, but of the strangest things: foreign coins, a shoe with a missing heel, a strip of cloth torn from the hem of a dress, rolled-up pictures of saints, all tied to infants that had passed through the wheel.

Where are they? I asked.

Figlia della madonna, the ruotaro said: in the hills with wet nurses.

IV

Albert Murray arrived in R. on a train from Montreal. It was early autumn, that's to say the autumn of 1921 or 1922. In the Rockies he saw mountainside after mountainside of black and grey spires; fires had climbed through the trees in the railroad's right of way. He arrived to find a river village surrounded by burnt forests.

He went to stand in the village fountain, to play the chanter he'd learned to play while working on the Montreal docks. He'd saved enough for his train ticket and a little more. Then his haversack had been stolen on the train. A young woman he recognized was kicking up road dust as she pushed by a barrow full of rags for the midwife. It was one of the last hot days of that year, dry, and the sun bowed her full shoulders. She held her proud, shy head to one side, listening to the reedy chanter.

Do you see this? It's not mine.

He had stepped into the fountain, chanter in hand,

motioning to the water. An orange floated there.

Do you think I've forgotten your name?

Lucia, she reminded him. The shy, curious glances between them said they had not seen each other for months. While he had remained in Montreal to work, she'd travelled to R. with the child Manice, to join her brother.

No Lucia, you can't have the orange to eat. Who knows how it got there? And she, walking toward him, said, So what? As if how it got there mattered now that she, Lucia, was about to climb into the fountain to press into him.

He stood in the water, pants rolled to the knees, and played on a single reed that made the frantic sound of birds she'd never heard of. It was his way of saying he'd lost everything, that he had no savings with which to begin their life here. Even his boots had been stolen on the train, and now he was cooling his feet.

I put the orange there, he confessed. It was all he had after the months of absence: something quickly pocketed in the dining car.

Where did that come from?

From the train.

You bought it? her eyes wide at the extravagance.

I stole it for you.

On the riverbank below the village, he was tapping a slateface with a hammer, spreading his hand on the grey face of the bank. He tapped once between thumb and forefinger, then pressed an ear to the stone. A keen smell of snow in the air seemed to come from the stone itself. In its song, the way healthy stone sings when you strike it, was a kind of soft laughter.

A muted light played on this stone that already smelled of winter; the slate shimmered in indistinct colours with grey edges. He tapped along the riverbank, listening and humming.

The slateface that went for a hundred yards in both directions hummed back.

High on the bank above stood Our Lady of Sorrows with its cedar shake roof. At his feet, a wide river. The slate he'd stacked on the sandbar was so sharp that it had split the rotten calf gloves he'd found in an alleyway.

The river frothed ice crystals. His fingers were going numb.

And there, the wide grey sky between the mountains, lean with snow, any day now. How the hammer's small voice rang against the cloud mass.

In his hunger, he rested against the slateface. A few grains of snow fell on his sleeve. The coat he'd borrowed from Lucia's brother was tight at the shoulders, his left hand numb.

What does rain sound like on the wooden roof of Our Lady of Sorrows?

On a wooden roof rain does a tapdance. On a slate roof it sings.

Here now, the booming grounds. Taunt ropes, three fingers thick and lashed to iron rings driven into the bank, shivered like violin strings. On the far side of the log boom he could see the D. Street sawmill at the mouth of the Illecillewaet. Through the clapboards, the gleam of the sawblade. A storm was blowing down the valley, and the grey-backed logs began to rock at his feet.

By the mill, three men and two horses were dragging cedar logs ashore. Now the men began to strip the logs.

They raised their arms high and the bark came off with the sound of tearing paper.

Lucia had taken him to her brother the village bootmaker. She walked ahead, eating the orange while he wheeled the rag barrow. She crushed the peel in her hands to perfume her hair, a childish gesture of happiness.

When they caught the extravagant fragrance, people in the street turned to her. She chewed on the crushed peel. A bell rang as she opened the shop door.

In the narrow shop with its odours of leather and beeswax, more like a darkened corridor than a room, boot moulds lined the side wall shelves. They were waiting on the shelves, unmoving. A pair were taken down. They rested in the bootmaker's hands like fat pigeons the colour of milk. They were asleep.

The bootmaker ran his hands that glistened with beeswax over their wings. They were like birds that slept in wells. At the bench he covered the boot moulds with a leather sheet. The leather was soft, subtle, indistinct in colour; it had been worked to exhaustion, and it shed the pale colour of buried asparagus shoots.

For the field inspector's wife, he said.

From a shelf behind the workbench he took down two or three pairs of boots. Try these, he said. The men who paid for them died in last winter's avalanches.

When does it rain here? the slater asked.

In the Fall.

And how long are the roof icicles?

Long, long, said Lucia. From the eaves to the snowbanks! Though he had only arrived that day, she could tell by his questions that he was already thinking about work, about the pitch that a slate roof would require in this new village under the mountains.

He walked across the log boom to the mill. The mill was silent. Rather than follow the shore, he walked straight across the two-acre booming grounds. Hungry, he touched some wild potatoes in his jacket pocket. A light snow was falling. Before setting out across the logs, he'd strung his new boots around his neck on copper wire.

Where the bark had been worn off the log felt slick underfoot. He used his toes to grip it.

You put the only food you had at your feet and you pointed to it. He hadn't kept the orange for himself. When he saw Lucia with the barrow, he immediately took it out of his shirt and placed it in the fountain.

There it was, floating, a poor joke for her.

And then he took out the chanter.

> *He made the sounds of strange birds, I tell you. Though he was very hungry he did not eat. It's there, he said of his only gift now that his haversack had been stolen. Help yourself.*

He went across the logs toward the mill. Sometimes only shadows were visible in the slanting snow, a short coat that flapped at his waist. In the mill the giant circular saw, choked with sawdust, gave off a soft grey light between the clapboards. When he fell on his hand, pain stabbed into his left elbow. How could he have fallen—hunger dizzy? He gave a cry, more of vexation than hurt. The three near a slabfire on shore stood up. He could see their gloves drying on stakes tapped into the ground.

You see he's fallen in, he heard one say. That was the boss Gio who the day before had refused him work.

The three left the fire to come to the shore, good. Now they would see what he could do: walk hunger-faint across the sleek backs of the logs as though they were the perlins of Our Lady of Sorrows. Yes, they would see that in his agility and confidence he was the one to replace the church's wooden roof with slate.

Asleep out there? the boss Gio shouted.

Now he was going toward the workers on shore, the short coat flapping at his waist, the slant snow blurring his eyes and lips.

They were stripping cedar logs for street light poles. While they rolled the poles onto the drey, he carried the bark to the fire in his one good hand, his left hand curling in pain and going numb from the fall.

Who will pray in your church? he asked slyly. Under a wooden roof? Who will do that for you?

He reminded the boss Gio of the dangers of a wooden roof in a valley where the sparks from the locomotives regularly set off forest fires.

On a wooden roof rain does a tap dance, he observed. On a slate roof it sings.

On the veranda steps she was dealing out cards she had collected by the tracks. Men played cards on the station platform while waiting for a train, or in the roundhouse at night, and she'd gathered those dropped on the tracks or flung by the wind.

Yours is the king of hearts, she said, watching him swing an axe in his good hand to split firewood. It had one torn corner like a dog that's gotten its ear chewed in a fight.

And who is this? she said wide-eyed, mocking, taking another card from the deck. A lady? And look how she stands, proud! Why don't you offer her your arm? But no, the king of hearts with his chewed ear, what does he do? He slips back into the pack and there he hides, too proud to ask for food.

She had said this while watching Albert Murray go into the cabin he'd rented from her brother, promising to pay later. To have been robbed of everything he'd saved angered him, and he wanted no help.

Crows flapped overhead while he gathered chestnuts. Lucia had shown him the abandoned field with the two trees in it. The chestnuts were wet in the dark grass and he had to feel for them with his fingers among the long tufts that were stiff with frost. This field, too, had gone a little way and then been abandoned. The potatoes he gathered were wild potatoes, bleaching along a ditch that had not grown over. Take that spade, she had said, her words ringing against the flinty ground as obstinate as he. Someone had planted the two trees, the field, and then gone on, who knows where.

He's dreaming of Lucia's lips, said one of the sawmill workers in the drey. He spoke of the slater who had fallen asleep stretched out on the snow-covered poles, his head lolling against the sideboards. The street had taken a turn to follow the high bank, the river below frothing with ice. On the drey seat Gio stood with the reins in his hands. He was gazing with pursed lips at the silvery roof of Our

Lady of Sorrows. He had supervised the building of the church and now he had doubts.

Her lips touch you, said the worker to the sleeping figure and the others smiled.

At a hole dug in the street, they awoke the Scottish slater to roll out a cedarwood pole for the street lights. Soon all the storefronts, lit up with kerosene lanterns, would have electric lights. It looked ready to spread the light in its newness, the tea-coloured pole stripped of bark.

He was no longer able to uncurl the fingers of his left hand. And yet he must work to live. In their cabin on second street, Lucia drew up two chairs and they sat face to face. He looked frightened and defeated, his nostrils pinched white from the pain. Their daughter Manice was asleep in the only bed.

What are our most beautiful birds here? she asked in a soothing voice. Two yellow finches came early in the spring, with bright yellow throats. Too early because the snow had not yet melted. Come outside, they called, empty your pockets. They had shrill voices like two tin pipes played against a wall.

I said to those birds, What do you want?

Threads, they piped, threads for our nest. They were in the chestnut branches by the King Edward Hotel. High up, two yellow stains, I heard them piping against the wall. I said, What do you promise me? They had the voices of dripping icicles. Thaw pain, they said.

From a high shelf she lifted down a cedar plank with the nest on it. Of woven threads and feathers, it looked like a watch satchel and it weighed nothing.

They had worked hard, those birds. She looped a thread through the nest mouth and carefully tied it to the fingers that Albert Murray was no longer able to uncurl by an effort of will.

The nest of threads hang from your fingers. What is held in there? Let its weight thaw your hand.

Already, an ice skin in the river shallows. He stood in the cabin doorway, a pair of antlers cradled in his arms. That must have been the autumn of 1922, their second in the village. She could smell the blood on the skullcap. The antlers looked like those dwarf oaks that, no taller than your waist, grow out of crevices and hollows near the treeline. The cabin was filled with the odour of her cooking. And through it all, like a bitter thread, the smell of the animal's blood. It must have been huge to bear those antlers. She imagined its eyes and the mist of its breath in its nostrils. He talked in his pride of winter meat, more than enough for seven families. He'd already given some to Mrs. Canetti down the street.

Those antlers, moss-covered, were heavy. He had them cradled like a stone in his arms; the points were spread by his face like splayed fingers. She had dreamt of this creature. In the dream the creature had come out of a forest of lodgepole pines in which the night slept out the day. It was very old. Two young deer walking alongside supported its head with the gigantic antlers. She remembered the two deer had milky blue eyes, for they were blind. And now the creature's antlers had appeared in her doorway, spread in her lover's arms. She felt then that he was unlucky. Something was going to happen to him. Maybe what he lacked was not luck but guile, the sly slipperiness some golondrinas have, those who smell trouble from a distance and who, when it arrives, have long disappeared.

The burnt-out spires that surrounded the village disturbed him.

"Where will we build our house?" Near the CPR tracks so that during the next fire they could run to the station, where a train just might happen to be waiting? Near the Western Canada Wholesale building that, surrounded by its shipping yard, looked like a place of refuge?

In the hills of Roca, she told him, there were often earthquakes, mudslides. You had to be careful where you built your house. To find a safe place, she said, you went into the church at night when the priest was asleep and cut from the hem of the alter cloth a little square this size, and she pointed to her thumbnail. This you put under your tongue. Then you walked your land. At the safe place to build, the alter cloth would warm your tongue. It would signal: Build here!

She went out into the snow hissing under the new street lamps. For the first time, the street that led past the storefronts to Our Lady of Sorrows was lit up after dusk. The after-dark light reminded her of a magic box that she'd seen in Montreal: you gazed through the peephole into a candlelit world, a street scene like this, with figures in windows and doorways, passersby. There is a man in an alley chopping wood; another is crossing the street to the movie theatre, with his lady. He wears a cloth cap and the woman has black gloves painted on her wooden hands.

Mackenzie Avenue lit up at night reminded her of a magic box, only she was in it. Light quivered on the faces of a passing railroad crew and it gave their eyes a fevered glitter. Their foreheads shone like mirrors; their voices sounded tinny and hollow, as in the Illecillewaet canyon. Outside the dome of light loomed the mountain. A locomotive's lights flickered way up in the high pass.

She felt a terrible unease as she withdrew to stand in the doorway of the Modern Bakery. She remembered how the magic box owner had signalled that her time was up. He'd brought his hand between the candle and the lens that illuminated the street, a suffocating blackness. How pale and waxen the passersby on Mackenzie Avenue looked as they strode arm in arm through the falling snow, now laughing, now transfixed by the electric murmer of the street lights and the cascade of light that filled the street. She felt like running, to claw her way out of the glittering light that settled on her eyes and lips like flour.

Albert Murray was at work on the church roof. He'd stripped the cedar shakes for kindling. Below, by the church doors that Lucia was painting green, were stacked slates from the Illecillewaet valley. He had not been satisfied with river slate. It was too soft, he'd told her, and would only last for sixty years. So he'd taken trains into the mountains, jumping out here or there on a high grade to walk up a burnt-out valley, an avalanche track, till he found stone good for a hundred.

A dark-green streak on her hand, from painting the church doors ferried upriver from St. Leon. The St. Leon boatbuilders had made these nailstudded fir doors a good ten feet high, to hang on steel hinges forged in the roundhouse at night, when the stewpot was bubbling. The doors were laid out in the churchyard on sawhorses. Three coats of paint for the summer heat and three for the knife-edged winter cold.

The mountain billowed over Our Lady of Sorrows in a blue, milky haze. The snowcap, thawed and refrozen, flashed like a mirror. There was blasting going on above the village, to lay a second line of track. A puff of smoke, rattling windows, sometimes the aftershocks and salvos shook the churchyard. A section of new track near the village had already been laid. She had walked on it. To the side were slabs and blocks of blistered rock, with scored dynamite tunnels. The raw stone, covered in blasting dust, smelled like stagnant water.

Now, many years later, I hear that young woman say, How quick things are done here! The frenzied building was like her decision to leave Roca, to get away overnight. She sees the swagger of the laid track, but also its fear, the inner trouble. The fear of remaining among the burnt spires that surround the village, the unsure place.

V

At dusk, the three-car ferry tied up in its moorings, my father cast for redfish long after they had settled into the deep currents.

I was sent to find him.

Supper! I called from the landing.

I could hear the line hiss as he made a cast, the lure strike the surface. A warm, still night, the air clear, flicker of village lights on the river. I climbed under the padlocked barrier, walked up the ramp to the deck that smelled of oil and iron rust. Off the stern, the shadow tip of the rod flicked like the willow wand Anna used to knock chestnuts out of the crowns of the trees.

You're going to have a sister.

Is Anna here? I said. I thought she must be asleep in the wheelhouse. I remembered how, since she was born, it was said she would be like a sister to me. I was five or six years old then, now I was thirteen, and I hadn't seen her often. Paolo didn't like his two families to visit the village; he kept them away from us. The stillness that I felt came not from the sky nor the mountain nor the river, but from my father's face under the peaked visor, his body a long shadow that goes rippling along the rod.

Anna! I called.

No, he smiled. Your cousin Maren is coming to live with us.

Hands under my arms, he pulled me to my feet.

We walked up the road through the village orchards. My father had placed the fishing rod and the tackle box in the wheelhouse. Anna was not there.

For a few steps he turned on the flashlight that he carried in his pocket.

Better, he said, turning it off, his hand on my shoulder. He'd heard the Hydro was going to build a dam south of Burton. In a few years our village would be flooded. We would have to move, and he was talking of building a house in the orchard above the takeline. The village houses and buildings would either be trucked to a new site or burned.

We could say we won't go, I said.

We have to go, he said, resting his hand on my head. They take what they want in the end. And we will get what we can from the Hydro, he assured me.

Still I remember something in his voice I'd never heard before—a far, dark drifting, like someone speaking out of a dream.

How will you trick them? I was remembering nonna's story of how the slater, dressed as a woman, had escaped under the eyes of the priest with the infant Manice.

I won't have to trick them, I'll show you.

The road went between slate banks, then through orchards to the takeline. With his flashlight, my father pointed out orange ribbons hung from surveyors' stakes, the heap of peach trees torn up to make room in the orchard for our new house.

Nostre nonna will be angry!

I remembered how she once chased me with a cedar stake when, climbing into a apricot tree, I'd broken a main branch. I tried to measure her anger from one branch to twenty or more trees and looked at my father in alarm.

Nonna gave us this land, he said.

For Anna's birth I was given new shoes. For Maren we were given land. I sensed his happiness, yet all I could feel in myself was alarm. The wide gap in the trees was darker than the mountain, and the churned-up earth smelled of broken roots.

I don't like it here.

You will, he smiled. When you have your own room.

Those words seemed to float without meaning: takeline, reservoir at full pool, own room. All I could think of was the castle, the village, the railroad bridge, and the Pradolini house across the river, all flooded. I imagined the reservoir foaming across the stump hills we used to call orchards, through the vineyards to touch the trees outside the promised bedroom window.

What if we drown?

This will be our orchard, he reassured me, above the takeline. Now that Maren is coming to live with us.

That's all I could do, ask questions, and I felt his grown-up impatience; I was only trying to call him back.

We asked a lot of questions in those days, questions for grown-ups who were off somewhere in some dark water, trying to think out where to go while our houses were trucked away or burned.

It was two days before the village *festa* that was to last a week. My father read a letter from Maren's mother. Before taking his early train to St. Leon, Uncle Paolo had slipped it under our door. I'd found the envelope, Don't Show To Nonna written on it—the thick letters scrawled on the envelope with a carpenter's grease pencil, in capital letters built out of lines that crossed, or leaned against each other like timbers.

Don't show to nonna. Yet she knew nothing and everything.

Before I could open the letter, my mother took it: Not for your eyes, either.

The letter lay tucked in its envelope on the kitchen table that my father pushed against the window as he said: Maren must come for the festa. My bed had been taken out of the laundry room, put by the big stove that we never used, the iron monster that clicked its teeth at night. "She must have her own room. A boy doesn't need his own room; a girl does."

The letter on the table pushed to the window to make room for Maren. Later I saw it among the copper-bottomed pots on the shelf above the stove. I wanted to read it, to see why the cousin was coming to live with us.

But in a way I already knew. Three days before, my uncle had arrived to sleep downstairs. Through the laundry room window, I'd heard him talking.

Good morning, mother, he murmured.

He spoke softly on the porch below. They'd brought out chairs so they could sit hand have their coffee. Nonna's would be half milk, warmed in a separate pot. I could hear the legs scrape as my uncle drew his chair in, to lean against the wall below my window. The porch, this house listened to you. No radio chatter, no ticking clock; the light and the smells listened to you.

I heard nonna say, So *she* has left you too? And what about my granddaughter?

Years later I found out for certain what my uncle was bargaining for that morning with a shy smile in his voice: a granddaughter in exchange for the Giacomo house in our village.

I'll have to take her away, he'd threatened. To the Aconcagua. *You give me the Giacomo house and we'll stay.*

It was then that it was decided: Paolo would get the house that nonna owned across the street. Because he was often away on the trains, Maren would come to live with us. I didn't know then that he was losing his eyesight, and he didn't either. Macular degeneration, the doctors would later call it. I took the way he looked at you out of the corners of his eyes as a kind of slyness.

My parents made Maren's bed in the room off the kitchen we called the laundry room. It had a double wash basin in it, a washing machine, a big window that swung open, with the clothesline outside. It used to be an open porch, with wooden stairs that led up to it. The trainmen used to leave their overalls and jackets on the stairs for nonna to wash. That's how she made some of the money to buy the Giacomo house given to my uncle. Now the porch was glassed in, with a window in the kitchen wall that looked into it.

In the laundry room my mother was standing behind my father.

Maren is coming to live with us, she murmured. Who will work when the valley is flooded?

He turned to her, a brief glare of anger in his eyes. We'll have the peach orchard above the takeline.

Who knows if you can ripen peaches on the side of a reservoir, she complained. She went into the kitchen, to pour a cup of wine. We should move to Westbank.

Westbank, my father echoed. He spoke again of the Hydro's unwillingness to pay anything but the "going rate" for our village land. It was worth much less than the orchards and vineyards of Westbank. I felt then that my parents' voices were adrift, that they'd slipped away into the place of their leaving.

We don't have to move, I told them, my voice uncertain.

And we'll end up paying taxes on lake bottom! my father shouted. His angry words rushed through my body as though I were transparent air. I crept behind my mother, a sound shadow.

I drove with him to the bus depot. Though the waiting room was empty, I knew with a child's logic that Maren was behind the photo booth curtain, by the twenty-four-hour lockers that you paid to use. She waited for the whirr of the machine to produce the strip of photos before she drew aside the curtain. Maren's bags were already by the glass doors: two suitcases with big metal locks. The depot smelled of floor cleaner and old newspapers. Because we were late, Maren was the only one left.

Pushing aside the curtain, she smiled when she saw us.

Her hair was cropped short. "I asked my mom to cut it!"

At the ticket counter, while my father carried the two suitcases outside, Maren asked the price of a return ticket to Field, wrote it on her palm.

She held up the strip of photos. Who is that? she said, pointing not at the wet photos, which she held pinched at a corner, but at herself. Maren, I said. I remembered the green eyes, slender chin; I had no trouble recognizing her.

Once again she went to the counter, to verify the price of a return ticket to Field. When the dispatcher spoke, she looked first to his lips, then to her palm, like nonna checking an address on a letter, number by number, word by word.

My father drove down an alley, through puddles from the heavy rains, by rain-stained cedar fences and metal garbage cans on stands to keep them away from the dogs and above the snowbanks in winter.

Maren's dim eyes; she reached for the door handle, lifted it. A twelve-button accordion rode in her lap.

You used to play in the Field *bassa banda*, I said, remembering.

We were riding in the back seat; my father had put the two suitcases on the seat beside his. Maren had been on the bus for most of the day.

I had a long day to get here, she said. On the bus she had sat across from a boy and a girl. At a rest stop she had seen the two, the boy, the girl, lean across a cafeteria table with their chins propped in their hands to kiss. They had leaned across the cafeteria table smiling and had kissed smiling with their eyes wide open, and it wasn't the kiss but what they exchanged with their open eyes that she remembered.

My mother has a room for you, I said, my voice full of resentment: she was to have my room, the laundry room. Now I remember the oiled floorboards, with cracks between them. If you put your ear to one, you could hear what was going on below. I used to listen to my uncle's voice. I had learned to predict when he would ask for money.

Her hand was on the lifted door handle. My father, who had heard the click of the latch, drove as if a load of firewood had shifted on the car roof. He explained that at the last minute the station dispatcher had ordered Uncle Paolo to take a train to St. Leon. He drove past the Giacomo house that nostre nonna had given Paolo; she twisted in her seat to gaze over her shoulder at the darkened windows.

A low murmur. Maren was singing to herself.

She had lifted the door latch. She could have leapt into the alley, the price of a return ticket written on her palm. Instead, Maren told me she'd never had her hair cut so short, that the cut had given her a different face. I remembered the last time I'd seen her, under the table during the grape harvest. She was four years old then. Between those tablecloth walls, I'd felt I was in my kingdom. A pale light shone through the cloth. On the roof, rain was the clatter of knives and forks. Voices were the voices of people in the street. She had slid out of her chair under the table. You have a long neck, she'd told me. Like a horse's. She smelled of cinnamon and diesel oil. She'd arrived in the cab of the Sentinella, perched on the sacks of cinnamon that my uncle used to dust his vines against mildew. I remember that her mocking smile made me feel trapped, no longer left to myself.

At fourteen, Maren wasn't tall for a girl. She had angular features and a downcast look under bushy eyebrows; she looked as though she felt singled out. She had the waist and hips of a young girl and so with her wrists. But she had a woman's hands and she hid her breasts under my mother's loose-fitting blouse. She'd begun to walk as though others had a *reason* for noticing her. That evening when I saw her coming out of the laundry room, turning to close the door, I thought she was a stranger, a thief maybe, for she closed the door like a stranger's door.

So that she wouldn't sit alone in her curtained room, she was made to do her homework at the table cleared after dinner. Papers spread on the table, textbook open, my father explaining a math problem, writing quickly as he spoke.

I'm one of those people that are no good at math, she said. The night before the festa, she wanted to talk about the albero: prizes hung at various lengths from the top of the pole; you kept what you reached and carried down.

My father looked astonished at what she was talking about. "We stopped that years ago." He turned away as though trying to recall something.

Well, you're from Field.

The next day, to announce the beginning of the festa *campestra,* it was custom to visit others in disguise. My uncle dressed up Maren as a man, with a tape-on moustache. She wore a plaid shirt open at the collar, baggy sleeves with rolled-up cuffs. Pant legs tucked into the big workboots she had on, so they wouldn't get caught in the bicycle chain as she rode beside my uncle, pressing the moustache to her lip. Her hair was piled up in my grandfather's hat from the cellar, with yellow tobacco stains on the rim.

This is my brother Antonio from the Aconcagua, announced Uncle Paolo. He had put a cap gun in Maren's pocket ("You're a dangerous character!"). They were visiting Mrs. Canetti, Maren's godmother.

Your brother, so young and handsome. And from the Aconcagua!

He's a tough customer, my brother; he's going to take over my business.

The *commare* was setting out plates of gnocci, two bottles of beer.

Your business, what business?

I sell blasting supplies on the side, commare, and Antonio here is telling me to be on my way. He wants to fly Bennello's plane, too!

Maren laid the cap gun on the table. Under the moustache, she burst out laughing. That day in the village she was the dangerous brother from the Aconcagua. For once Maren seemed free, in her element. Now and then she pressed the moustache to keep it stuck on, over her eager laugh and wild gestures with the cap gun.

Once, to calm her, my uncle placed his hands on her shoulders: You behave yourself here. Stay by your nonna, who is rich. And then, with a puzzled look: When I look at you straight on, you seem blurry. When I turn my head to the side, I see you better.

That night—the night before the madonna was brought

out for the parade of decorated fruit cart—there was a fire and music on the Illecillewaet sandbar. Maren and I went out there. We were tolerated by the older teenagers who were making plans of mischief for the evening.

Who would you like to go out with, one of the older boys asked me. His girlfriend was toying with his idle fingers in her lap. Others laughed: He's too young.

Maren, I said.

All of a sudden the stillness in their looks, the cedar crackle in the fire throwing off blue flames.

A joke, I blurted out.

The next morning, my uncle pulled Maren by the arm down the alley.

Don't you shame me, he said, and he lifted her hand to see if any of the painted handprints on the fences matched hers.

Once after school Maren and I happened to walk home down an alley of high fences of weathered board. It was as though we were walking in the Illecillewaet gully, with the strong sunlight reflected from the wind-polished boards and the smells of rotting garbage from the cans on wooden stands by gates that, taller than a man, were always closed. Maren tried to remember the houses on the streetside, to figure out whose we were walking by. In those days she was a liar. She told me she had a knife her father had taken after she'd buried it in the head of a dead raven. Or that her father, who had moved to a different town, was going to send a picture of this woman he lived with. At the pink stucco wall of the Community Centre, I pushed her down: My uncle is your father. Everyone knows.

Okay, she said. And this, too.

She would go into my parents' bedroom to look through the dresser drawers. She took out my mother's jewellery box, the folded bills hidden under it, the old razors, the railroad watch that no longer worked, the folded ferryman's shirts, the panties, the one crumpled tie. And replaced them as they were.

Once my mother watched from the doorway.

Later I heard her say to my father, when she thought I was asleep:

She wants to belong here.

Dressed as a clown Maren wore my grandfather's slouch hat, a taped-on moustache.

On that bicycle, she pedalled past looks that said: The daughter from Field.

They made her eager to play the fool. Once she sang in a hurried, breathless voice:

> Girl guide dressed in yellow
> This is the way you treat your fellow

※　※　※

The next morning—the third or forth of the festa—nostre nonna said to me, Bring the dill for the madonna's cart.

All winter the dill was kept in the cellar. On the cellar stairs I saw that water, glittering with coal dust, had welled over the first three steps to meet me. After the heavy rains of the day Maren arrived by bus, nostre nonna's cellar had flooded. Now as in previous years, when the water vanished I'd find salamanders in the mud and shrimp that lived in underground streams, translucent with pepper grain eyes. Crouching, I made glittering trails in the coal dust on the surface of the water. A raft of grape lugs and cedar bolts had floated from under the stairs where I'd built it in the winter.

The echo of wine bottles under the light by the furnace. I pulled the raft in, untied it, poled with a broom handle along the wall. Ripples slapped the stone walls, and water came up between the slats as I poled the raft over to the shelves. Reach down the dill fronds from rough cedar shelves above the highwater mark.

The house is dying, Maren. Already it refuses us.

At night I hear waterfalls in the cellar. I see smoke stains on the windows.

The house had settled during the night, creaking like the ferry in its slip. That morning my father's shirt sleeves and hands were covered in shavings that had the odour of cinnamon and old oak. He was planing the doors stuck in their frames.

My father called from the top of the cellar stairs: Anna is here.

She came down to the step above the water in a dress with patch pockets, a sunhat. Don't worry I won't kiss you, she said, and she did—a cousin's kiss. Under the plaited brim of the sunhat, I saw dark eyes, flashing teeth, someone who, over winter, had grown almost as tall as me.

Maren's living here. Where is she?

I said she was with the priest, to get ready for the parade of the madonna and the trip to bless the new graveyard above the takeline.

I haven't seen her in a long time! Do you think she'll recognize me?

Yes, I nodded, uncertain.

What if she doesn't remember me?

Just say your name, I said. Just say Anna Esposito.

We climbed the stairs into the kitchen. I laid the dill on the table. My father was sitting by nostre nonna, brushing wood shavings from his hands. They were discussing the land buyers sent by the Hydro.

Try always to have a friendly witness around, my father recommended. Offer wine, our braided bread.

My uncle, his voice full of anger, was talking about the Hydro machines in the vineyards last evening: Their drivers say, Sorry. We weren't sure about the fence line. They trample fences!

A little grape sugar in their tanks, he suggested with a sly look.

Talk about everything under the sun except the business at hand, my father countered. Never allow two of them to discuss business with you alone.

He passed to nonna a Hydro brochure that showed holiday cabins on the shore of the future reservoir, which was advertised as a recreation area.

They lie like the priests, she said.

That day of the madonna, of the trip upriver to bless the new graveyard, we stripped the window frames to paint them for the festa. My father was on a ladder, scraping the blistered paint with a tool shaped like a claw; a snow of heavy flakes fell into my hair, my eyelashes. The different clothes I put on, the various colours of my hands: green of the church doors, pale violet of our windows. The dust, the paint flecks in my hair like flakes of many-coloured slate, chalky dust smeared across my forehead as I wiped away the sweat, holding the ladder for my father. He was two storeys above me, and I couldn't look at him.

They say not to paint, he says, hooking the claw tool on a rung. That painting our houses for the madonna won't bring us more Hydro money.

This isn't for money; this is for honour.

All these years later I can still smell the burning dill. It had a sweet smell, the grey smoke that drifts on the river while my uncle plays his yellow *zerocetti*. The dill torches hiss as they strike the river among the flowers sent out for the festa.

My grandmother said, You come with me. I had never seen her look so determined; her cheek was white, as if she'd received a slap. She'd slipped a pair of kitchen shears into the pocket of her black dress. This was after I'd brought the dill from the cellar and after she'd slid the Hydro brochure across the table.

At the foot of my uncle's house across the street, I knelt to peer into the madonna's shrine, the size of a birdhouse made of slate. My uncle had found her in the 1923 avalanche. Twelve years old, he'd brought the madonna down the mountain under his coat: She's the only one I saved. Orchards south of the village were being cut down for the new dam, and a pall of smoke rose there. The madonna wore a blue robe that draped her arms above the upturned palms. Her high, rounded forehead. I tried to imagine the eyes under the lids, once pressed in snow like flour. A pale plaster showed through her chipped fingers.

While nostre nonna knelt to clip a square of silk from the hem of the madonna's blue robe, she muttered under her breath:

And the sickle is not a hoe
Not a hoe the sickle
There are those who uproot and those who plant
Those who plant and those who uproot

For you, mother, she said. A song from Roca. My gift for your gift. It was the song she used to sing in the ospizia to the infant Manice. She would sing it at night to calm the baby against the priest's footsteps, full of whispered hope to get away. Now she struggled to her feet, the square in her fist. I wanted to know what it was for. For you, she said, raising a finger to her lips to say quiet, no more questions. From down the street we could hear the creak of the picker's cart, many voices.

A red silk thread tied around her wrist, Anna carried long dill fronds that quivered as she walked. In the street of the grandmothers, my uncle wheeled a picker's cart with the madonna on a bed of straw and grape flowers. Others joined in from behind their gates as he walked to the ferry landing. He'd slung his yellow accordion with its buttoned bellows on one shoulder. The Canetti family waited behind a gate and by custom it was the grandmother who opened it.

Come place a gift: a handful of grape flowers, a ribbon in the cart, a loaf that smells of saffron. My father was waiting at the landing, the low rumble of the ferry's engine. Six girls of the village, Maren among them, carried dill fronds and lit candles along the gravel river road. The gravel clattered in the heat. The fronds dipped above them, like pale sputtering flames. Maren had powdered her eyebrows and fingers with grey ash. In her open shirt she smelled of sweat. Green eyes and slender chin—she walked at the side of the priest. I saw her eager smile. With the five at the side of the priest, she was far from Paolo's silencing glance. She wouldn't look at me. She wanted to be left in her element, the ceremony itself. She looked like she belonged. Anna with her lit candle was behind; she was talking excitedly to the candle-bearer at her side in a loud, cheerful voice that I could tell was meant for Maren, who wouldn't turn around. I could tell each was aware of the other, though nothing was said between them.

Out on the river, we passed below the railroad bridge. I remember that we were going to the new graveyard that the Hydro had made above the takeline. We were going to hold a ceremony over a plaque for the seventy-six who had died in the 1923 avalanche.

Wait, my uncle said: Once their mouths were full of snow; soon they will be full of water!

My father's ferry had turned upriver into the strong currents, among whirlpools capable of drawing a log to the bottom before releasing it. At middeck, tables from the firehall were laid out with salads and gnocci, roasted ham, and braided bread. The accordion music went out like smoke, awake and dreaming, travelling low across the water. To have a feel for the currents, to feel your way along as a blind hand glides up a bannister.

We passed beneath the railroad bridge, and Paolo brought nonna a plate of salad and gnocci.

I won't be eating with you, she said brusquely. I've burnt my throat with tea.

Anna looked at her, sensing there was more to it, and said nothing.

Go see a doctor, my uncle advised, if you've burnt your throat like that. He placed his accordion on the table, offered to drive her to the clinic when we returned to the village.

She pushed away the plate he'd brought her. I'm fine. She stood to walk to the stern.

You come with me, she said, biting her lip.

Off the stern we could see the churning prop water, the railroad bridge with its catwalk of cedar planks, the green haze of the Pradolini orchard on the far shore.

You are my only grandson.

Yes, I nodded.

I bought the Giacomo house for you. It was meant to be yours.

She pressed the blue square from the madonna's hem in my hand. When you go to look for your new home, put this under your tongue. It will protect you.

Maren had joined us. Nonna wet her kerchief with spittle, to quickly rub the priest's ash from Maren's nostrils and from under her eyes, those round peering eyes that smiled at the old woman. You two look after each other, nonna said.

I saw Maren draw back then, flushed to her hair. She gave me a quick, bewildered look. She took Anna's hand and the two walked away to the middeck tables where Paolo was uncorking wine bottles.

Now I see the grandmother's words had named a distance between us we were unable to cover. Our automatic reaction was to fly from each other. The cousins at the middeck tables were laughing and whispering, and I had the impression they were making fun of the way I stood rooted at the stern, embarrassed and exposed by the words of the old woman who loved us. I had no idea of how to look after either of those cousins, and yet I was drawn to them both. From where I stood, rooted by the grandmother's words, I could see that they were watching me, mocking and distant. Later, Paolo would take me aside to ask, What did nonna say?

Now that he'd bargained for the Giacomo house, he always wanted to know what the grandmother had to say outside of his hearing.

The metal railings shook as the ferry slowed to turn ashore. Once we had landed, Anna strode away and stood on a high sandbank.

I'm going to see the new village, she said, turning to look over her shoulder.

It was hot where we had landed. There were some cottonwood fibres caught in Maren's hair from the trees over the sandbar. A path led up to the new graveyard. I remember trying to search for mocking laughter in Anna's eyes, a reaction to our grandmother's words. She said to no-one in particular: Me and my sister are going to see the new village.

Maren hoisted her shirt to show me a bottle of wine she'd taken from the crates under the middeck tables and in her knapsack a carton of ice cream from the icebox.

Me and my sister aren't going with the others to the new graveyard.

In the new village I saw Maren sprawled on the curb outside Bruski's store, which was on the blocks used to move it there. Over the past days the Hydro had moved buildings and houses from our village to this site. Soon many would live here.

Got to get up, Maren said, but she didn't.

Anna was propped against a chestnut sapling. The street was empty, the windows of Bruski's store sheeted in cardboard. As she went to pass Maren the carton of ice cream, she scraped her knuckles on the bark.

I saw then she was drunk. Because of the wine, she didn't seem to feel the pain of the scrape, nor did she notice the blood welling on her knuckles.

Why don't you get down from your bicycle, she said with a wave of her hand, and help us.

Maren, who was on the other side of the trunk, roared with laughter.

Jumping bean, she cried, wiping the tears from her eyes. Jumping bean get a grip. She was no longer wearing her loose-fitting blouse; she was wearing Anna's cowgirl shirt braided up the front, with studded cuffs. Maren had gone over the fence to Bruski's to take a wild rhubarb leaf that looked like a star cut from wet tissue paper spread in her lap.

First off your bicycle, Maren repeated, though I had walked here as the cousins had from the ferry. Why are you staring? Did you follow us?

The ferry is loading, I answered. Time to go back to R.

Those places are from R, she said, pointing to Bruski's store, the Fuscaldo house, the Swede's house. But this isn't R.

Not R., Anna echoed, the corners of her mouth trembling with mirth.

And then she imitated our grandmother's voice: You two look after each other.

He can look after himself, said Maren, turning red.

A clear mid-afternoon light had settled on the pavement, clean as a pressed sheet. When I knelt to lift her, Maren shut her mouth and tried to compose her look, yet her lower jaw trembled. She smelled of wine. She dragged a wisp of hair across her lips and bit it, to keep calm. Only, her eyes had begun to water.

I have to pee, she said.

Crouching, Anna lifted her. We went down the street, past houses from our condemned village that were still on blocks in the air. There was a high flush in Maren's cheeks and a brightness to her eyes. Anna was almost as tall as Maren. When she laughed there was a certain gladness in her voice. Walking back to the ferry made her stop laughing, made her wipe the tears from her cheeks. My sister, she said.

I saw Maren didn't like being called *sister*; she gave Anna the look of someone slapped, as if she too felt the distance between *sister* and what we really had, between *new village* and a site strewn with uprooted houses and stores, blind windows sheeted in cardboard. It gave me a giddy feeling in the chest, the sense that we could float away anytime.

Early the next morning, all the laundry room curtains were drawn. To call Maren, I rapped softly on the laundry room glass. I carried a chair across the floorboards to the iron stove, to reach down the letter hidden among the copper-bottomed pots.

On the cellar stairs I crouched above the water stirring against the walls.

The letter said:

For one thing she is too lonely.

I felt her breath.

Maren had come down behind me.

Why do you want to push me in? Turning to look over my shoulder, I shoved the letter into my pocket.

I felt her breath. I don't want to push you in. I can't sleep here; it's not like I remember. What were you reading?

A salamander had surfaced at the foot of the stairs, its head a dark aspen leaf. I reached for the net tucked by the stairs, made out of a nylon stocking strung on hanger wire.

Nothing for you.

The cellar light held it to the surface, wide black eyes. I turned the net inside out to free the struggling body with its flame-coloured belly. It thrust its snout into the little hollow between the curved thumbs of Maren's cupped hands.

From the cellar stairs, we could hear my uncle's accordion in the street of the grandmothers. He was the *bassa banda.* He played "The Dolphin," "Grass," "The Black-headed Saint."

That's your father, I reminded her. It was the third or fourth morning of the *festa campestra* and he was waking everybody up.

She told me what she remembered from six years ago. She remembered the albero hung with prizes: Salami, mortabella; money and toys disguised as bunches of leaves; and at the top of the pole the grand prize, a young lamb that had been slaughtered and dressed for cooking.

I haven't seen that in a long time, I said.

We took the salamander to the river. We went down

the alleys to avoid my uncle's cheerful accordion. She had opened the gap between her thumbs to look into its glittering black eyes.

Listen.

Cranes were flying over the village to the southern flats; their wings made the sound of slowly revolving helicopter blades.

Maren had stopped in her tracks.

Cranes, she said.

There were hardly any songbirds, although crows flew restlessly from chestnut tree to chestnut tree. We went down the river road patched with gravel. The cranes were dropping into the river like an uncoiling braid of hair. On the Illecillewaet sandbar, while she slipped her hands into the river,

I stood back to read:

> She ran away to Nakusp last week. If she had had enough money, she would have gone on to Vancouver. We believe there is no point in forcing her to stay with us any longer; it will only make her more miserable.

※ ※ ※

Maren and Anna flattened their hands on our kitchen table, to show that their thumbs curved in the same way. You see? We have the same father! Anna was demonstrating the use of a willow wand to knock down the highest chestnut clusters: "You have to know how to *do* something here." Alone, neither of you walked away from me. Together you were mocking, distant. The dog-eared strip of bus depot photos in Maren's pocket. "My hair is already longer; It's curly like yours."

I'd read from the letter I'd stolen:

> *She's a bright girl, but she's too unhappy to*
> *concentrate.*

Do you want to run away from here?
I've always wanted to live here, Maren.

To prepare for the last days of the festa, we children were gathered in the church basement. A nun in a black and grey habit described all the toys in heaven. She was directing her remarks to the younger ones—ages five or six—who, wide-eyed, heard about the dazzling, irresistable toys of heaven. Maren shook her head in disbelief. She bit her lip, glanced from side to side. Later, when it was discovered that the money collected in the madonna's plate had been stolen, the nuns put us in a line, palms up.

Hold out your hands.

When the ruler struck, Maren made a fist, more in panic than in anger; she refused to let go. The nun tried to shake the ruler from her fist. Maren's eyes were full of wild panic. Turning to flee, she tripped over a chair and split open her chin. I remember her look of helpless panic as she examined her bloody hands. She ran to a door that opened onto a staircase leading outdoors. The nuns rushed after her. I saw that, expecting me to follow her, she'd stopped at the door. I edged behind the rushing nuns and the taller children who were staring in disbelief at the blood pouring from her chin.

I climbed around her in the high branches.

Hi! Fine!

She told me she was fine before I asked her.

You have to go to the St. Leon clinic, I said.

Crouching below me, shirt pressed to her chin, she said, Sometimes I have this feeling I shouldn't be alive.

My father's shouts guided her down. Call the doctor! he shouted, though he knew it wasn't the doctor's day in our village.

I slept on the way down and woke up in the streets of St. Leon. I don't remember the doctor who arrived to unlock the clinic door, turn on the lights. In the operating room there were pads of blood-stained gauze in the sink, implements scattered across a metal tray on the counter.

Climb up then, he said, his voice full of sleep. He spread a clean sheet on the table. He quickly draped a sheet over Maren's chest. He wrapped her arms in the sheet, then tucked the ends under her back. When he sponged her chin, she began to cry, staring at the ceiling.

I'm ordered to hold down her knees.

The doctor, impatient to return to bed, doesn't wait for the injected anaesthetic to work. For the first two stitches she winces, lips clamped between her teeth, her face bathed in tears. Her knees, trembling under my hands, feel like wood.

I didn't question what the doctor demanded of me; I held down her knees. There was nothing else I could do. By her amazed, staring eyes and her reproachful look, I felt my stomach hollow at the shame of that betrayal. Now, many years later, I understand these things: to hold down her knees, to jump to that order, was to make myself less than I was. When he missed a stitch, the doctor swore, pushed through the sickle-shaped needle. He wiped away the disinfectant, dabbed on antibiotic cream, then taped on a dressing that had to be replaced every day. As he gave his instructions, Maren, free of the wrapped sheet and sitting on the table, continued to stare at me with astonished, reproachful eyes, the look of someone who sees you as you've never been seen before.

She doesn't do her chores because she's unhappy. She lies about it so she won't get into trouble. Then we bawl her out; for that she builds a wall around herself so it won't penetrate, and so she won't get hurt. After it's over we all hate each other, and the work still isn't done properly.

Under an open window through which I could hear the trains, my father reworked his house plans. He was sitting at the kitchen table, drawing by lamplight. I was in bed: a fold-up cot that my mother brought out at night, made up. I watched her step over the low sill, to sit with her bare feet outside on the warm porch roof shingles.

My father got up to rap on the laundry room window. Through the drawn curtains you could see the light from Maren's reading lamp.

He rapped again softly: I've something to show you. His finger traced across the house plans.

This will be your room, he said, on the first floor.

She was wearing my mother's flannel pyjamas and her feet were bare. Her hair, which had grown longer, was tied at the nape, and she had a gauze dressing taped to her narrow chin, under the wide, green eyes. She smelled of cinnamon and disinfectant.

She had her new look: cheerless, resigned. From my bed I heard her say, I can't stay here.

Of course you can stay with us, my father said with surprise. You're tired after the shock of your fall. You need to rest.

Through the window over the sink I could see that across the tracks the train station was lit up: the passenger train was arriving. It would stop for an hour, then go on to the coast. My father called it the Vlanmore train. Italian immigrants once took that train from the transatlantic docks of Montreal. Where are you going, they asked each other. Some were going to Vlanmore, others to Sanmore, others to Windamore. But they all got off here at the same village, my grandfather among them.

Sometime in the last days of the festa campestra, Paolo came into our upstairs apartment from the roundhouse, with the yellow zerocetti on his shoulder. That accordion was made in Castelfidardo in 1910. It was tuned slightly sharp for the sake of brilliance. In his arms he carried a copper brazier from St. Leon. It's cold in the Giacomo house! To warm his room at night he'd burn almond shells in the brazier. There was a little metal shovel to stir the coals.

He asked for nothing, though now and then he gazed at Maren. He touched the dressing on her chin—a caress that was also a reproach.

Maren had never heard of the Aconcagua.

"It's a mountain in the Argentine." He described the vineyards of his childhood, watered by the melting snows, and the vast grasslands. He spoke of peach trees that grew so quickly they were used for firewood, of the Barletta wheat and how you had to plow not three but six inches deep so that the rockless soil would retain sufficient moisture. I saw Maren's eyes squint, as in a glare.

He carefully unfolded a map before my mother and father, tracing a railroad from Rojas to Mendoza.

You take the Rio Cuarto from Mercedes.

Maren refused to play "The Red Rooster" on his accordion. A pale light shone through the window onto the table where my uncle had placed the copper brazier.

Play Carpani's "Moonlight." Once again she shook her head, eyes lowered.

She won't play for her father!

And why so often then did he say "she?"

Look at her, how she is eating!

Look who she is asking.

He pointed in her science book and laughed: How do you know____?

Well, because . . . and Maren explained. She held the book open before his hands.

You can do all kinds of things, she told him, leafing the pages to show him.

I can't see those blurry lines.

Maren hated math, but she knew more chemistry than any of us and this made her proud; she spoke hurriedly.

Paolo said she was "showing off."

He touched the side of her plate: Your mind is elsewhere.

"Thank you!" In the midst of his words, her mind was elsewhere. She was wearing a light blouse that my mother had given her, full at the wrists.

I was waiting for Paolo to ask or tell us, and now he spoke: Today I lost my job on the railroad. My eyesight is going.

Do you hear me? he repeated. Do you hear me? He had the yellow accordion on his lap, still buttoned, and at his elbow on the table the copper brazier glowed dully in the late afternoon light.

My parents, who were still looking at the Rio Cuarto map, rose from their chairs. My father placed the science book before him: Show us.

I turn my head to the side, he said, I can read fine. I look straight at the page, all I see are blurred lines.

I didn't believe the shy, faraway smile in his voice. I was sure it was another trick of some kind.

Anna Esposito. When I think of that name, my mind wanders. Nine years old, she was the only girl left on the school field. A late afternoon under a cloudy sky, long shadows on the field. In order to keep her attention, but to show that she would not be let in our game, we made up names for ourselves.

Vince Berutchi called himself Ochi.

Peter Alfi: Scusso.

I was called Tulip.

The game went faster and faster; we played without looking at her. That was on the school playground, under a cloudy sky in 196_.

Anna called out, Who is looking at you?

You're looking at us, I said.

I'm not looking at you.

Then who is?

Tulip is looking at you.

What's your name? Vince asked.

Tulip! she decided.

While her influence over us grew, she remained quiet. Even our laughter sounded blurred; we talked too fast. I remember her standing at the edge of the school field, always with that mocking flicker that never left the corners of her mouth. Her wide, quiet eyes reminded me of a salamander's. Now she had a worried look as she twisted a finger in a lock of hair behind her ear.

Come with me. Tulip wants to talk to you, she said. I followed her off the field, to stand by the playground swings.

I was in the Giacomo house today, she said, and I heard Paolo tell the land-buyers he'll sell the Giacomo house to the Hydro.

The swing chains were creaking in the wind that came up from the river. The seats, cut from truck tires, turned and weaved like driftwood under the bridge.

He's going to the Aconcagua; he's taking Maren with him.

Did you tell nonna?

Yes, she said. But Paolo told her he's not going anywhere. You gave me the Giacomo house, he says, and I'm staying.

VI

That Fall Manice lost her house. It was around the day my father took the ferry across the river for winter firewood. He carried his two axes, his chainsaw and a gasoline can to the landing, early enough so that the Cancelled Sailing sign hung on the padlocked gate wouldn't bother anyone. We were going for cedar on the other side, burnt-out spires from the 1930 fire that had leapt the river, burned lowertown.

I don't see how it could have happened. I look at the river, wide with the colour of a sky massed with snow—and I say, How did the fire cross?

There used to be a shake mill in the cedar grove on that side, I remember my father saying. In the summer of 1930 a fire started in the slash near the mill. It was so small that no one paid any attention. The village was more worried about the forest fires to the south, which had filled the valley with a haze that turned the sun blood-red. One afternoon the wind picked up. Within minutes the fire had spread from the slash into the mill yard. Wind-driven, it roared from the storage sheds to the mill, and it flung burning shakes like handfuls of leaves across the river into lowertown.

Anna and I left my father in the pilothouse. We ran from bow to stern, coats flapping in the unusually warm wind. Anna high-stepped as she ran, making the clop of a horse's hooves on the deck.

The ferry landed, my father walked into the cedar hollow. Anna and I climbed through nostre nonna's orchards to clean out the Pradolini house for the golondrinas who would arrive later in the day. I found a broom to sweep the leaves from the porch; we carried out a kitchen table that had collapsed on its legs and boxes of newspaper and wine bottles from the cellar. In the yard by a chestnut tree was a bathtub of tea-coloured water, streaks of rust on the chipped enamel rim. We played that game Anna liked, travelling from room to room on the counters, abandoned bed frames, and furniture without touching the floor. Anna loved to climb. She was sent into the crowns of the old chestnut trees, to knock down clusters with her willow wand. My uncle would guide her down with his shouts.

That afternoon the golondrinas moved into the Pradolini house. For the harvest they crossed the river at dawn, on a catwalk under the railroad bridge. After the last ferry run, they'd use the same catwalk to return to this house. Because she was worried that one of them might fall in the river, my mother gave them watered wine at supper—a late supper at dusk at tables of planks and sawhorses under the trees outside the vineyard gate. They ate, drank, carried hurricane lanterns over the river. The Calabrianne was among them. I remember her vigorous strong face, the tight braid of grey hair at her nape, the way she laughed when, under the peach trees where nonna had spread a black dress for me to lie down on, she heard of the shoe I'd pushed out the car window.

Sometimes my father offered a ride on the ferry, which the golondrinas refused. Sometimes ten or twelve lived in the old Pradolini house, workers nonna had hired for the harvest. While they ate supper at the plank tables, I would listen to their Quebecois French, their Italian and Portuguese. Once I heard the Calabrianne sing in her high plaintive voice:

> Blessed virgin
> I met a man and a woman
> bound in a ball of yarn
> water flow thaw pain

Later at night from my bed, I saw lanterns on the railroad bridge.

The river brought their voices that I heard clearly without understanding, voices brought close with a ringing and an echo in them like the sound of a bell way down the valley or up the mountain.

That autumn, the autumn of 196_, the Hydro took Manice's orchard at the south end of the valley and bulldozed the house into its cellar. Beneath her orchard the hillside was gouged into levees for the new dam. The earthmoving machines had cut terraces to her fences. Though she was paid valley prices for her land, the word we used was "taken."

After a rainstorm, I remember watching her peach trees sway and tremble as though they were trying to walk. At first I thought they were wading through the earth, till I saw that the earth was moving with them, yawing in deep cracks to the pit below.

To stop this, my uncle had brought out the madonna to stop this, a little blue doll with chipped fingers. He carried her among the half-buried trees. I remember the silence—all the birds, terrified, had fled. He placed her in the branches of a young apricot tree, reasoning that at least to save herself, she would not let any more trees go over. Among the apricot leaves, her eyes were the colour of fir pitch. When you tapped her side she sounded hollow. We could feel the low murmur of the earth and how Manice's house had begun to tremble; you could hear stones falling from the cellar walls.

Terrified, Anna climbed into a chestnut tree near the house. High in the branches, she clung to the swaying trunk. My uncle had to climb after her to bring her down.

Why did you sign? Why didn't you make up an excuse? Why didn't you say you couldn't write or that you hurt your wrist! screamed my uncle.

Manice held out the court order the landbuyer had brought; my uncle snatched it from her to read that she had to be out within a week.

The day Manice moved to the Pradolini house, we crossed the river to help. Ears white with calamine lotion, Anna took my father by the wrist to show him her garden, a small fenced garden with a magnolia tree in it that smelled of warmed olive oil. She said she didn't want to move to the Pradolini house, the house of the golondrinas.

Where will we go from there? she wanted to know.

When my father had nothing to say, he wore a kindly expression to mask his worry and lack of knowledge. A wind was flowing down the banks among Manice's orchards, carrying the smell of the warmed land at dusk. All the lights in Manice's house were off, and a lot of the furniture was heaped on the porch. Nighthawks, diving over the river, made a hissing sound with their wings.

Nighthawks, he said, to take Anna's mind off the house of the golondrinas, the house she was going to move into. They hunt by sound!

Anna went to bicycle around the house that was to be burned down, and she sang:

I don't want to go.

I don't want to go!

Stones falling from the cellar walls made the hollow clop of a horse's hooves. She rode swinging a rope through the dangling clouds of mosquitoes till she came into the porch light flushed, licking the salt on her arms. Sand crusted under her nose as she drank water from a baby food jar—all the glasses were packed.

Let's run together, she said to me, then went to sit on the porch to pulp some berries, a lavender hand trail dotted with seeds. "We used to make money from these."

Anna, what are you doing?

Turning on the lights.

No, not in the middle of the evening, Manice said softly from the porch table. Anna, don't *interrupt* us. Go play now.

I remember my aunt's pale, anxious expression, and the way my father knelt on the steps to listen.

Go play now.

One light off and one light on, Anna said in the kitchen, turning on the light over the stove, the alcove light.

I'm the ruotaro, she said brightly, watching her mother. I've come to take all the people who are never home for supper.

As long as we're here, I said, the machines stay away.

Today, many years later, I remember how things would go. First, the drivers of the earthmoving machines would splash the house walls with diesel fuel to set them on fire. Then they would use their machines to push the smoldering wood and stone into the cellar and blade it over with earth. They were powerful, those Hydro people. They had machines that tremored the earth under your feet, a schedule of things to do that took all the light of recognition out of their eyes.

I remember the landbuyer at the kitchen table, tugging at his cufflinked sleeves to straighten them, the flash of the tiny gold links over the court order. He talked of land values in the valley, of what land like Manice's had gone for in St. Leon and in Renata. And when Manice asked where she'd find orchard land elsewhere for his price, he smiled, spread his hands to say, That's for you to decide. We've bought from others you know: Bruski's store, the Giacomo house. He walked through the house, measuring rooms; he counted the trees in her orchard; he saw money in all that, underwater.

☙ ☙ ☙

That autumn, after she moved into the Pradolini house, Anna started school in late September. Lost in the hallway, she wandered into our class.

I pretended I didn't know her. I was afraid she would shame me.

Isn't that your cousin?

I shook my head, bent over my desk, gazing at the wood grain till I became absorbed in it, all forehead. Dimly I could hear their laughter. Others had turned in their seats to say, Don't look at us!

Anna stared at people. Lost in looking, my father called it, or *gathering wool.*

What is your name? asked the teacher, Mogliani.

Mumbled words.

Speak up child, what is your name!

An-na es-*pisi*-to!

General laughter; to hide her face in her hair, she lowered her head. Our teacher took her by the hand to the office.

When he returned, he wrote on the board:

figlia della madonna

He told us of the famous wheel of Naples, through which many, many children were passed. I remember his words: And what were these children named?

Innocenti. Esposito.

Our teacher Mogliani was from Naples. He told us how lucky we were, that almost all of the infants who went through the wheels of Italy died in the first year, many thousands of them.

You are as rich as kings, he said.

Rich because alive? When people say things like that to you, you don't know where you are. Many laughed. We knew most of what we had was to be taken by the Hydro.

I never knew when one of the cousins would show up in a way unconnected with my life. By appearing in our class doorway, Anna had singled me out for ridicule. I can still hear the mocking laughter of my classmates who saw my unwillingness to acknowledge her. She was four years younger and I didn't want to see her in school. I felt she was from a different life, that she didn't belong there.

That day after school, I saw her crouched in the alley behind the Community Centre. With a stick in her hand, she was prodding thoughtfully at a grey cat under the Centre's fire stairs. In shadow, the cat glared at her, its tail twitching. She didn't look at me, even when I crouched beside her.

You can come with me to nonna's, I said.

They all laugh at me!

Not if I'm with you, I promised.

VII

I got up before dawn for the festa campestra.

My mother was making coffee at the gas stove under the narrow alley window. From my bed by the stove we called "the iron monster," I watched my mother make coffee before she left to deliver the bread by cart horse in the street of the grandmothers.

Uncle Paolo is ashamed, I said.

Yes, she nodded.

In our village, when a man for some unknown reason didn't show up for work, we would say he was "ashamed." Now that he'd lost his job on the railroad, Paolo delivered bread by cart horse in the village alleys. She'd seen his dogs outside the King Edward Hotel, where he drank at night. She delivered the bread when Paolo was ashamed, in order to make money to buy land in Westbank.

I must have slept through the baker's call. I stayed in bed, half-awake, and through the open window I could hear the whistle of the yard engine as it put together cattle cars for St. Leon.

The Sentinella was in the roundhouse. My uncle used to take the Sentinella to St. Leon for the zucca melons.

From the river I also heard the whistle of my father's ferry, announcing the first morning trip from the far shore.

There was a ringing in my ears, like a voice in a tin pot when someone dies. I sensed that my cousin Maren was still in her room. I had awakened from a dream, the print of her kiss on my lips. And the music: the distant wail of an accordion in the orchards under the mountain, a ribbon of her tone that, lifted from the vineyards and the orchard floors, brings the odour of dusty leaves and ripe fruit. With the imprint of her kiss on my mouth and the taste of cinnamon, I draw the sheet over my head.

I struggle against the odours of wax and bread, of violets and horse dung.

I feel my mother's hand burrow under the sheet to find my shoulder, my cheek, that she touches with fingers that smell of coffee.

Paolo is ashamed.

I see his two dogs outside the doors of the King Edward Hotel, where he drinks at night.

The warm fingers that touch my cheek make the kiss vanish.

I heard my mother leave through the back door in the laundry room to pick violets in the garden, to tie to the horse's halter before she harnessed it to the bread wagon.

The last time Paolo was ashamed, I'd helped my mother package the bread in wax paper that you folded around the loaves, and then there was a machine in the bakery to seal the ends with heat. It left wax on my hands so that they gleamed as though polished as we loaded the bread crates into the wagon. We went down the alleys early in the morning, when the air was heavy with the smell of dew from the mountain, heavy and still.

My mother wore a broad-rimmed hat of plaited straw.

She would bring the horse to a halt by drawing her hands together, or turn it up the alley by drawing the rein gently along the neck. Once she said, Would you like to learn music?

In exchange for our looking after Maren, my uncle had offered accordion lessons.

I'd heard him play during the first night of the festa. Outside the Giacomo house, I'd heard him play "The Rooster."

To save our condemned village, the St. Leon fishermen had brought a fishing scow upriver, their papier mâché San Calogero with its great almond eyes at the bow. At the head of the procession walked the Calabrianne. As she walked by the Giacomo house, Paolo struck up "The Rooster." He was sitting in his second-storey window, lit up by a lamp at the far wall.

For her, he played "The Rooster."

The paper San Calogero followed behind on its bed of grape leaves, a mantle flung over its stiff, outstretched arms.

The Calabrianne smiled as she passed under the music, and she made a dance step. Then she returned to her solemn posture, and the coil of knotted hair at her nape no longer trembled.

I went out to decorate the orchard below Butucci road. A

withered apricot struck between my shoulder blades, and I knew that Maren and Anna were in the trees. A warm breath stirred around the trunks, with its odour of leather and rope. Now and then, far off in the alleys, I could hear the voice of my uncle's accordion. I heard Maren's laughter in the crown of the trees, a track of gleaming prints that vanished. Nonna was at the trestle tables, where women were spreading the gnocci, the braided bread. She came over to touch my forehead:

You've a fever!

She made me sit in the grass beneath an apricot tree. From another table came the Calabrianne. She opened a blanket that smelled of smoke from the barbecue pits for me to sit on. Her breath tasted of the young wine they were pouring at the trestle tables.

Are you staying for the dance?

In the long hours before the dance, the Calabrianne wore a Calabrian dress embroidered at the chest. She spoke to nonna in Italian I couldn't understand. She said she was one of the golondrinas.

That bird, the insect-eater that you often saw on the river at dusk, skimmed the water and dipped to drink. I had never touched one and now I touched her inner elbow. I had often caught the finches we called the gra-peaters, to toss them high over the nets. How could she be one of those birds?

Will your mother dance?

Paolo is ashamed, I said. My mother would have to deliver the bread and help the baker later in the day. Maybe she'll be too tired to dance.

Even now I'm not sure of her name, but we called her the Calabrianne.

In the apricot branches and leaves that were coated with dust from the new reservoir, I'd fallen asleep and dreamt of the wail of the Sentinella on the mountain, of the throat of the zerocetti that trailed its voice like a ribbon in the street of the grandmothers. I'd tied festa streamers in the crown of a Butucci apricot, to hiss over the trestle tables in the late-afternoon wind from the river.

You come down. You forgot to drink, said nonna, touching my forehead. Go home to bed. Fell asleep! What if you'd fallen? Nonna stood at the trunk. She pressed a wet cloth to my lips.

Go to bed.

On the street of the grandmothers, I kept under the chestnut boughs, by surveyors' ribbons that marked trunks to be cut down for the new dam. Were it not for the weight of my hands and eyelids, and that of the strange buzzing in my ears threaded by the voice of my uncle's zerocetti, I felt I'd float away, vanish over the high-beaked snowplows by the roundhouse. While I climbed the steps in the castle to our apartment, the voice of my uncle's yellow zerocetti grew stronger.

I'll teach you to play.

I didn't like the accordion's harsh unpleasant voice, tuned sharp for the sake of brilliance. He left it on the kitchen table and led me outside by the wrist. We sat on the wellhead. He smelled of the cement he'd mixed to cap the village graves. Now that he no longer worked for the railroad, he'd also taken the job of cementing over the village graves. He'd made a plank keyboard, with whittled hollows for the bass buttons. The plank went between knee and chin, this one up and this one down, he said, tapping his fingers on the wood.

You try.

I could tell that he didn't want to teach me. He spoke in a low voice about the vineyards of his childhood, the ox skulls that were used for chairs in the workers' huts, the ox carts whose wheels were solid wooden discs as tall as a man.

Who do you think will come to the Aconcagua? Do you think Maren will come? The worry in his slumped shoulders and the fear in his glance made me draw away from him.

She wants to stay here, uncle.

With his thumb, he was rubbing the dried concrete from his palm.

Is the zerocetti grey or is it yellow?

Everyone knows it's yellow.

One of my eyes says grey, he said. The other yellow. You tell my daughter that.

Why?

I need her to go to the Aconcagua with me. To see the place where I was born.

You tell her, I said.

Anna danced before me like a cat. For the festa she was wearing one of nonna's dresses from the cellar, and it smelled of coal dust and cedar. She had a dark green streak of church door paint on her hand.

Who's behind me?

In Maren's room the yellow zerocetti cleared its throat. I could smell its bellows of strong manila cardboard and its soft leather gussets. It was dusk. My parents were still in the orchards.

Go on, Anna said, look through me.

In the laundry room doorway, she danced before me like a cat. I felt the low bass chords in my chest and in my fingertips, and I could smell Maren's odour of cinnamon.

Try to go through me, she said.

Anna wore my mother's lipstick on her bright, fixed smile and mascara smudged under her eyes. When I went to touch her, she was not there and then she was. "He wants to take her to the Aconcagua." When I pushed through, I heard her whisper, She doesn't want to go.

Maren made the accordion say I had a long day to get here; I walked from the Butucci orchard. She was playing the accordion on her cot.

Did Paolo give this to you? she asked me. She made the accordion wail like the Sentinella and laughed.

For as long as I could remember, I'd heard that whistle on the mountain, usually at night, when Paolo used to take a train to St. Leon for the zucca melons.

It woke me up; it was like a familiar footfall in the stairwell and a voice I knew.

We're going to the Argentine, she said. Do you want to go with us?

Yes, I nodded.

She reached up to rub my face with her hands. She talked of the Aconcagua till her eyes shone. Her laughter was like a track of wet footprints on warm floorboards.

They don't have a real San Calogero in St. Leon, she said. Just a papier mâché one. Do you want to come to the Aconcagua?

I want to go with you.

There isn't enough rain there.

How do you know?

Paolo told me. Why won't you look at me?

In truth, I couldn't look at her. For the first time, in the presence of her quiet stare, her excited patter, I was surprised by the tightness in my throat at the thought of her leaving.

Through the window I could see girls peeling zucca melons on the platform of the canning factory across the tracks. Maren made the whirr of many wasps, then a bird's flapping in the vineyard nets. She played and the Sentinella was in our room—I felt its whistle vibrating in my chest. Last night the Sentinella had whistled on the mountain and I'd heard the clatter of my uncle's boots in the street of the grandmothers as he went to meet his favourite engine. Even today I think of how she was playing at going to the Aconcagua, playing a child's tune on the accordion. Anna's saying she wants to stay here was dressed for the song she played, and so was the mascara smudged under her eyes, the worried, tight smile.

That night in 196_ was the last night of the festa campestra. In the Butucci orchard, my uncle had come into the firelight. "Where's Maren?" To turn a trussed lamb over the barbecue pit, he wore a leather apron and a bright red handkerchief tightly bound about his head. You could smell the grease burning on the coals.

On the street of the grandmothers, walking to the Butucci orchard, I'd heard her tone that filled my head with the scent of her skin. Soon, I was no longer sure it was Maren; maybe it was the wind in the river alders, under the bridge, the chattering catwalk, the streamers in the crowns of the apricots trees. As he stood in his greasy apron, staring around, Paolo did not seem to see me there. In the firelight he had the wide-eyed look of someone peering underwater.

I climbed through the branches near the barbecue pits.

Her hair smelled of cinnamon. She had tied streamers to the crowns of the trees. From there, under the street lights I could see that buildings that used to be in town had vanished: Bruski's store on Mackenzie Avenue, the Giacomo café. This place that was ours was rapidly vanishing. The streets, the lights, the orchards with their odour of ripe peaches, and the smell of the canning fires— all that expressed what I now recognize as the temper of our life was being removed, before my eyes.

I heard her voice in the leaf shadows: I don't want to go to the Aconcagua. Her voice among the leaves was plaintive and wide awake.

Are you going to St. Leon tomorrow? I asked her. On the Sentinella?

I edged along the branch, to kiss her on the mouth. She had climbed to string lights above the trestle tables. I felt the softening of her lips, their acceptance, then she pushed me away. In her hate-filled eyes there was a memory. Her look reminded me of how, while the doctor sewed her chin, I'd held down her knees.

I don't want to see you anymore, she said.

I don't want to see you again! she dropped from the branch to the ground.

When you're in a room, I'll leave, I shouted down at her. And when I'm in a room, you leave. With both hands I gripped the branch. I could have fallen when she pushed me. I hadn't chosen to help the doctor, I reminded myself.

Yet my shouts rose from the hollow feeling of being seen as less than I wanted to be.

The next morning Maren helped my mother wrap bread.

Wake up! On my face I felt the cousin's warm hands that smelled of wax. It was just before dawn and we went through the kitchen window to sit on the porch roof.

I'm running away, she said. I don't want to go to the Aconcagua.

Why don't you just stay here?

I don't belong here.

I could see a light flickering in the second-storey window of the Giacomo house. That room faced the mountain and was cold even in midsummer, with its walls stuffed with newspapers and sawdust. To warm his room, my uncle had lit a heap of almond shells in the brazier he kept there. Maren was carrying the twelve-button accordion slung on her shoulders and a small cloth knapsack.

I'm going away now.

We climbed down the chestnut tree by the porch, through the dusty leaves shaped like boats.

Hidden behind the trunk, she gave me a tired smile. She made the low wail of the Sentinella on the mountain.

Soon we heard the clatter of my uncle's boots in the street of the grandmothers.

You wait here, she said, and watch for Paolo.

She went into the Giacomo house, climbed the stairs to the room with the flickering light in it. I remembered Anna saying on the school playground, He's going to sell the Giacomo house to buy tickets for the Argentine. And I also remembered his promise to our grandmother: *You give me the Giacomo house and we'll stay.* In Paolo's bedroom

Maren found a trestle bed of faded green dealboards, the rolled-up mattress at one end. On the floor a copper brazier was burning. It gave off the bitter fragrance of almond shells.

Do you think he'll try to take me with him soon?

I don't know, Maren.

She fingered the carved headboard. She wasn't often in that house. On the day after she'd arrived on the Field bus, Paolo had taken her there to have her dress as a man. That's the only time I ever saw Maren free and in her element: the "dangerous brother from the Aconcagua," she pedalled beside my uncle under our grandfather's cloth cap, pressing a fake moustache to her lip.

Now I see her draw the brazier to the bed by one of its looped handles wrapped in cord, to tip out the burning almond shells.

Hi Anna!

She called me Anna as I climbed into the cattle car.

Frost gleamed on the rails in the shadow of the canning factory. Last night I'd brought her a blanket.

Where are you going?

Maren sat on a mattress of burlap sacks. Light streamed in through the cattle car slats.

Aren't you going to the Argentine?

No.

Paolo says when he finds you, you're going to the Aconcagua. Are you running away to Vancouver?

Yes, she nodded. Nearby, girls were peeling zucca melons on the cannery platform. Inside the cattle car I could hear drawknives make the melon skins hiss like split stone. The tasteless juice glittered on the knives and on the fingers and elbows. There was ash on the tracks from the Giacomo fire.

Everybody's looking for you.

You're going to tell them where I am, aren't you.

Though I had brought a blanket to the cattle car, she had not slept under it; all night, through the cattle car slats, she'd watched the red glow of the Giacomo fire.

We slipped by the factory platform heaped with melon rinds where the drawknives flashed. Crossing the tracks, I saw Lombardy poplars glittering behind the train sheds and the wide beaks of the snowplows.

Through a side door we crept into the roundhouse. That morning I felt I was seeing everything for the last time. Dawn streamed through chinks in the roundhouse walls, through the banks of dirty windows. Arc lamps blazed over the tracks, lighting up the empty cattle cars.

The roundhouse windows had turned the colour of river stones. To let out the Sentinella, the doors would swing open and the big engine would creep into the yard. Through the windows, you could see the shadows of empty cattle cars that smelled of sulphur water.

In the cab of the Sentinella, Maren explained the many levers. I didn't really listen to what she was saying. For the first time, I felt what it would be like to leave that vanishing place of my bones, my hands and touch. And now I speak of what I remember of the roundhouse that morning:

She went in through a side door and I followed. A pot of stew was bubbling on the stove by the door. High above, the wooden beams were covered in dust; light streamed in from banks of encircling windows. A worker was pressing a flat metal bar to the grinder at the far bench. Sparks flew under his goggles. The Sentinella stood by another engine that we called "the Tall Musician" because its whistle sounded like a deer bone flute.

In the cab of the Sentinella, Maren commented on the purpose of the many levers: "I've been in here lots." Between us there was a strained smile. She talked in a low solemn voice of the Aconcagua till her eyes shone. She spoke of how in one year, twelve sets of twins were born, of the wide river Plate, of the Mendoza earthquake that the French geologist Bravard had predicted.

That's not you, I told her. That's Paolo.

You're going to tell them where I am, she said with her resigned look. Aren't you?

In her eyes I was still the doctor's boy.

VIII

The train, rattling and swaying, crossed the railroad
bridge and climbed into the Pradolini orchard. Through the
cattle car floor I heard the voice of the wheels that asked
for nothing, a reassuring clack. On the ridge track that led
south through the valley orchards, I smelled canning fires
and wind-fallen, rotting fruit. Through the slats I could see
across the river to the glittering tin roofs of our village and
the D. Street mill at the mouth of the Illecillewaet.

I had never been south of Burton. Yet I could smell
the Kootenay Lake, the packing crates on the St. Leon
wharf, the rail car barge that brought in Renata fruit—all
things that my aunt Manice had told me about.

I can walk all the way around Paolo, Maren was saying. She wore a pleated, cream-coloured blouse that had
no warmth in it. I can walk all the way around him like
this, she said tracing a circle in the cattle car straw with
her toe to show the limits of his sight.

In our apartment, she'd pocketed a handful of peppermints that my mother liked to keep in a blue bowl on the kitchen table. I'd filled my pockets with *ciambelle.*

Now she gave me a mint: Put it under your tongue to make it last. We hadn't had anything to eat since the afternoon before the Giacomo fire, and she hadn't slept all night. Peppermint on her breath; I felt her lips tremble under mine. All around us was the smell of dry straw and urine. She'd made a mattress of burlap sacks among the straw bales that were used to pack the zucca melons.

Under my tongue, at the root, I could still taste the burnt house. I'd watched the flames climb out the second-storey window to curl into the eaves. I'd waited till the roof shingles began to smoke and then ran. Too breathless to yell, I went up to my mother, who danced in the Butucci orchard, and pointed to the red glow above the village roofs.

The clang of the Our Lady of Sorrows bell and then the fire truck's siren. My father drew the hose from the fire truck bed as though he were casting wildly for trout. I could hear the shouts of men over the fire's roar. At the yellow and red-painted hydrant on the street of the grandmothers, my uncle spun the brass hose coupling. I heard the cough and purr of the fire truck generator as arc lamps lit up running figures in front of the Giacomo house.

Paolo knelt to connect an attack hose to the main line, dragged it to wet the smoking walls of the adjacent houses. I heard windows popping, glass shivering into the Giacomo yard. Now my uncle and my father carried the attack hose through the front door, only to be driven back by the smoke and heated air. I saw my father, head ducked, raise his hands to cover his singed ears.

I can still smell that house. It stank of charred wood and sawdust, a bloated mattress dragged into the street, burnt plastic and linoleum.

I'd taken a bottle of drinking water from the fire truck, filled my pockets with ciambelle at our kitchen table.

You haven't slept all night, I said to Maren. You rest then.

I sat cross-legged, to cradle her head in my lap. The gleam and dim of her fingerprints on the water bottle. Through the cattle car slats I could see the river.

I listened for her slowing breath, felt the heartbeat in her fingertips. I stroked her hair, her minnow features. To breathe, our grandfather had cupped his hands before his face as the avalanche snow flowed like flour around him. Clawing to break the suffocating ice that his breath made in the little cavern around his nostrils and mouth, he wore his fingers to the first knuckle.

I wondered what death I might bring her. It's not only birds that feel the death in our hands.

Wait, my uncle once said to me: What does a man have for himself when he has lost himself?

A fist in the mirror!

At age five, Anna had drawn a picture of the ruotaro, a gap between the black hat and head and one between his body and the horse. Now my hands repeated that gap above her closed eyelids, her throat hollow with the locket in it. I dared not touch her. I felt then that we were unlucky somehow, that it was not only houses and orchards that were vanishing, but a tenderness that needed a place of its own. My head resting against the slats, I heard the thrumming of the train wheels. On a high grade they slowed to a clack. Through the slats I saw familiar trees: peaches and apricots pruned by her hand, the light between the branches as distinctive as a signature. That was Manice's orchard above the tracks. She let no one touch her trees and did all the pruning on her own. There were the trees I'd known since the age of four, and they were always pruned that way. Where Manice's house used to be, smoke trailed from the bladed earth. A ground-moving machine stood in the clearing; its raised blade, dirt-crusted and as long as a wall, gleamed like a weapon. I heard my uncle's low voice: *A little grape syrup in their tanks.*

IX

Many years later Anna told me how she heard the story of our grandfather's death. She heard this story two days after the Giacomo fire, when Maren and I had disappeared. She and nonna were in the castle's backyard garden. Our grandmother was telling her how the slater had gone to help dig out the seventy-six buried in the snow. While he and the other rescuers were in a trench they'd dug to open the tracks, an avalanche began on the mountain opposite. It could have been started by a shout when another body was discovered, that of a Chinese cook. The face of the mountain fractured. The slide quickly turned from white to black as it ripped up soil and flung timber spears, filling the rescue trench.

The village heard its roar from thirty miles away.

Nonna had crept into the street of the grandmothers, into a stillness that said they already knew.

Now, A plume of sprinkler water travelled across the

backyard porch at her feet. She cranked down the faucet handle. The hose vibrated shrilly, stopped. She told Anna she wanted to see who was out on the downtown sidewalk that evening. A familiar dip of the head, the right sort of cloth, a step that vanished in a crowd. It was strange how the slater was beginning to return to her in this way: the glimpse of memory in the way a hand rested lightly on a child's head.

That morning she'd been to the doctor about the burning in her throat, the dull old coin in her cheek. Folded in her pocket was a medical report that talked of the surgical removal of bone and muscle, at her age.

At her age!

Returning from the clinic, she'd seen someone who looked like Albert Murray standing in front of the theatre, cap pulled low over his eyes and one hand resting on the head of a young girl. The child was wearing a sundress with patch pockets. The man's clothes were not Albert's, she would tell me later. He was Albert in build, in the set of his shoulders. He reminded her of how young Albert Murray must have been when she knew him. He must have been very young.

The gate unlatched, she and Anna stepped into the alley.

She touched Anna's forehead with the back of her hand. You seem hot! Head bent, with dull glazed eyes, the cousin was listening to something inside herself. She had not left our grandmother's side since the Giacomo fire.

Where are my cousins?

Down in Burton, our grandmother told her. They were hiding in a cattle car. They'll be back tonight.

The yard engine was pushing boxcars together: the

clang of the warning bell as the engine backed down the track, the metallic echo as the boxcars engaged. Hand in hand they walked down the alley. She wondered if she would see the slater again. Not all the cedar wood fences were as high as hers, and she compared gardens, looking for something new: today a child's wading pool, the evening sky reflected on its surface. Passed the bowling alley, then boarded up, turned by the King Edward Hotel.

She and Anna went to rest in a park by the tracks. A strong light was spreading across the snowfields, high on the mountain behind the train sheds. She watched Anna hop over the tracks, to a young boy who was sucking water from a squirt gun handle. That was the Butucci boy. He was five or six.

Anna said to him, bent over, If you eat seeds and swallow lots of water, a garden will plant in your bones.

The children had walked beyond the tracks to the station platform. And there he was again, a figure on the platform. Nonna remembered when he'd gotten a job painting the station. That was the last day she saw him, over forty years ago. He'd come banging through the screen door with two paint tins hidden in burlap sacks that the train crews used to wipe down the engines. Isn't it a pretty yellow? He pried the lid from a tin of station paint. He went into their house. He started moving what little furniture they had in those days into the centre of the room. The walls were a dull whitewash they'd lived with for over a year. When they could no longer see how the paint was going on, they laid down the brushes and went to sit on the porch to drink wine, passing the cup back and forth. It was an unusually warm evening—like early summer. He cupped his hand on her belly, waiting for the kick of their second child. She heard the wail of the D. Street mill calling the night shift to work. The alley gate had been left ajar. From the porch steps, they could see the Community Centre, all lit up. Women in groups of two or three were strolling by the gate, to follow a snow path to the *Gioco De Lotto* at the Centre. The air was still, and as they passed beneath chestnut trees, shadows streamed down their fine cotton coats. How elaborate their hair had been done up for the Lotto. There were no men. The men were in the bars or working.

Some women had stopped at the gate.

I've found work, Albert said.

Give us your luck, they said arm in arm, laughing. Come and touch our cards with your luck.

He had the fine, nervous gestures of a small man trying to make room for himself, and she was not used to them yet. She took his head in her hands, held him in her gaze, seeing him again for the first time. Such a fine lovely man, she'd breathed then.

From the park bench, she watched Anna and the Butucci boy vanish in a hollow beyond the tracks. She stood to follow, to see where they were going. The fading light was turning the gravel between the tracks a deep blue. There were so many rails, narrowing and confusing her steps, but the pleasing colour of the gravel and the figure on the platform drew her on. She heard the warning bell of a yard engine backing down the line, but paid no attention. The strong vibration at her feet told her something she was too tired to understand.

Earlier that evening the Burton police had called to say two kids had been found in a cattle car.

Did she know them?

In the end, she tells the ruotaro, I've not been able to escape you.

I've not been able to keep anything.

X

Two nights after we were brought back from Burton, I was standing on the castle's porch roof. I was watching the procession led by my uncle's tractor with its aircraft landing lights. All the village cars and trucks were lining the dirt runway south of the village. My cousin Anna, ill with appendicitis, had to be flown to the hospital in Naramata. The cars and trucks were shining their headlights on the dirt runway so that Bennello could see where to land.

I saw a fire across the river near the railroad bridge. First my aunt's house, then the Giacomo house, now the Pradolini house. Through my father's binoculars, I could see Manice's and Anna's belongings heaped under the orchard trees beyond the garden and the yard. In the yard stood one of the Hydro's earthmoving machines. It would wait till the house collapsed and then push the remains into the cellar.

Earlier that night my father had come over to my bed: Anna's not feeling well. I'd felt the grip of his hand on my ankle to awaken me. He was wearing his ferryman's uniform: the grey pants with the black stripe, the blue jacket with the provincial crest on the shoulders, a cap with a peaked visor.

Do you want to come?

I shook my head.

Better, he smiled.

I had gotten out of bed to watch him polish his shoes in the foyer, a few nervous passes of the cloth. Nonna is downstairs, my father reminded me—as he always did when he knew Maren and I would be alone. "If Paolo calls, you get him to speak to her."

My mother was going with him: Anna has a high fever, she whispered.

I could hear a shower drumming on the metal roof. I knew that nonna was downstairs, but each time they went out at night, my parents told me this.

Now and then people called after-hours from the other side of the river.

If my father knew them, he couldn't refuse. "They wait for me. How can I sleep?"

Usually he was in bed by ten o'clock. I could hear the radio, a reassuring murmur and no light from under their door.

A call about Anna had come from the Pradolini house after midnight. It sent out a stillness into which we awoke, listening. My father got out of bed to answer.

Never once did I see him angry at an after-hours call.

Though once he refused to start up the ferry.

Sleep in your government car, he shouted to the agents who, on the other side of the river, were sent to demand the Pradolini house.

I was watching the cars and tractors on the flats south of the village. With their headlights on, all the cars and trucks from our village were driving onto the southern flats; the brightest were the aircraft landing lights on my uncle's tractor that he used to hunt deer at night on the Georgia Bench. Overcast sky, no stars. From above, the low drone of an airplane. Bennello dropped through the clouds, circled overhead, then skipped onto the lit-up runway.

Panic in my throat, I climbed through the window into the kitchen.

I rapped on the curtained laundry room window. Maren helped me to find an old pair of workboots in the foyer, gardening gloves, a torn pair of my father's pants bagged for the Salvation Army, a plaid shirt from the back of the closet, our grandfather's cloth cap from the cellar. To make the boots fit, I stuffed newspaper in the toes.

I won't go with you. She knelt to roll the pant legs past my ankles. Two they'll notice.

I looked down at her. No-one in those days would have called my cousin Maren beautiful: she had Roca D'Avola features, the look of a peasant girl from southern Italy. And when Mrs. Canetti stopped her on the street of the grandmothers to comment on her looks, she said. From Roca, and laughed because Maren's bushy eyebrows, her widespread eyes and the shape of her mouth made it easy to see where she was from.

Maren didn't push by angrily.

Yes, commare.

The grandmother asked to see her without the kerchief, to see the full effect of the wavy hair.

Last night Paolo had tried to come for her. Through the laundry room window, we could hear my uncle's voice on the porch below. I no longer have the Giacomo house, he bargained with our grandmother. You give me money for the Aconcagua and maybe she can stay.

Nothing more from me! our grandmother shouted at him. You want to take her away from me in my hour of prayer! She must have pushed him, because we heard his boots stumbling down the steps. Go away from here!

While I filled a sandwich bag with sugar, Maren stood at the telephone by the foyer door. Yes, during the first festa that I can remember, I stood at the telephone by that door. Anna, no more than a toddler, was sleeping alone down the street at her commare's.

Let's not wake her, said my father.

On that day our table was heaped with packages in bright cloth to be tied to the *albero della Cuccagna*, the trussed lamb that was always secured to the top of this greased pole, the braided bread. My mother and father were making the packages out of grape leaves while my uncle tried out some new tunes on his yellow accordion. Manice, nostre nonna, and Mrs. Cannetti were in the vineyards, picking handfuls of grape leaves for the madonna's cart.

It took all night to make the gnocci, the braided bread.

It took all morning to decorate the madonna's cart with ribbons and grape leaves.

Now and then my father would signal me with a glance: Listen.

I picked up the receiver; the commare's phone, too, was off the hook, so that should Anna awake, I would hear her cries from down the street. Silence, like that of someone listening to us. On the other end of the line, someone who was holding her breath to take in everything we said.

Walking down the street of the grandmothers to the railroad bridge, I pretend that everything I see is already gone.

> *Pretend that everything is lost, nostre nonna urges us.*
> *Only then will you see the true face of things.*

I take off the boots to feel my way along the cedar catwalk on the bridge. For luck, I touch the sugar bag in my pocket. Up here, the river's breath feels cool; the bridge smells of creosote and old steel.

I see our grandfather, the ruotaro, taking off his boots, crossing a log boom to ask for work. Even the snow-muffled voices of the men on shore are carried far.

Who brings you food when you're completely alone, traces your lips and eyelashes with her hunger?

He must have been very hungry, our grandfather. He'd gotten off the immigrant train with an orange hidden under his shirt. Everything else he owned had been stolen. The first thing to do was look for strong boots: for the dust track they called a street, for the mountain and for the riverbank that had slate like Anjou slate. The first thing to greet him in our valley was that bank of slate below me, and he talked first to the stone in a voice that says, I am recognized by you.

What was that sound?

A nighthawk, I imagine Maren telling me. So close, a sudden whirr in my ear.

I hear my grandmother murmuring:

> Not egg the lemon
> The lemon is not an egg
> There are those who uproot and those who plant
> There are those who plant and those who uproot

This is the golondrinas' catwalk, remember? The ferry tied up at night, this is how they returned to the Pradolini house that was now on fire: a path of cedar planks on the railroad bridge that chatters as you walk over the river. All the warnings that come from wood: the crackle of a chestnut branch saying you've climbed out too far, the crackle of a fire in a house saying run, run! The warnings that come from snow: when our grandfather Albert Murray climbed to the 1923 avalanche through the firs and pines, he heard snow packets dropping from the moss-draped branches onto his horses.

Below, the river shimmers like a dragonfly wing; its own breath a mist that hovers over the sandbar and on the village flats where all the trucks and cars are lined up.

Maren had stopped me on the porch, her warm breath heavy on my lips.

Hurry, she said. Some things needed the two of us to find them; the two are the reason they're felt. At night our windows were open. They were escapes.

Above, the creosoted ties, the steel rails. A hand to the rail above, you can feel the Sentinella from a long way off, more a feeling than a sound. I was on the catwalk, halfway across the river. Already I could feel the heat of the Pradolini fire as I walked toward it. One by one I saw the village houses, shimmering like breath. I heard popping windows, the fire's roar in the Pradolini eaves. I saw the gleaming blade of the earthmoving machine raised high in the trees. Behind me in the shadows on the castle's porch roof, the scarred chin, gentle green eyes: Sometimes I feel I shouldn't be alive.

Not that many years ago there was an unusually dry winter in this valley. Hardly any snow dusted the mountain forests, and in summer the reservoir retreated to the clear river channels. To prevent dust storms, the Hydro seeded the valley bottom with fall rye, and I walked out in the green fields between the river channels to find the village foundations. Here you can see the foundations of the Giacomo café, there the crumbling, silted walls of "the castle." It's all there, and in memory I trace the streets, the gravel river road, lines in my palm. I only see Anna or Maren now and then, at weddings or funerals.

Last year I saw Maren at her own wedding feast. She'd married one of the Fuscaldo brothers. I remember the boys of the Fuscaldo family; they were so polite and wanting to please. By the end of the wedding feast the father had tucked his chin to his chest, asleep, almost drunk. But it was the sons, the three of them, who kept up the chatter at the wedding table for the girl who had married the youngest. And you could see where she was from, in the shape of her face and lips. Maren stood tall above her seated husband, though she was no taller than a girl, her slender arms covered with freckles, and on her wrist she wore the bracelet her young husband had given her, a thick band of gold. She wore it as though it were a leaf that had fallen on her wrist and that she'd tied it there with a strand of her own hair, some girlish trick she'd forgotten, so that the leafy wrist went up and down in the conversation, knocking wine glasses on the table as she reached in her laughing for some plate to pass among the boisterous brothers.

The girls the two older brothers had with them were as polite as they were. They didn't laugh boldly with their mouths open. If they laughed at your teasing or your jokes, it wasn't laughter at all and they weren't going to lean half over the table to pass you some plate you wanted, not at all the kind to get out of their chairs and display themselves like that, with that gold bracelet negligently banging around things.

Then Maren calmed the Fuscaldo boys with a Roca D'Avola song. She sang a few words at the end of the wedding table and they sat listening, quiet in their chairs, astonished looks on their faces: where did *that* come from, that song, and they felt the thrill of it growing on them in their chests.

What we don't forget is like distant music. It stays with us, a song in the air to thaw pain. The valley bottom is no longer the place of certain words that have abandoned us. I offer this signe to our children; may it guide them under the tongue.

Acknowledgements

The song on page 79 is from Danilo Dolci's *Sicilian Lives* (New York: Pantheon Books, 1981). The songs on pages 32 and 52 are excerpts from a Sicilian harvest song published in *The Journal of Peasant Studies*. Excerpts from this novel, in a slightly different form, have been previously published in *Venue* and in *Queen's Quarterly*.

For their help and encouragement, thanks to Kit, Deane, Dion, Adrian, and Kegan; to John Taylor, Steven Heighton, Michael Winter, Edna Alford, K. Schmidt, Alison Watt, Ian Ross, Joanne Whiting, and especially to Tom Wharton, Ruth Linka, and Erin Creasey at NeWest Press. I would also like to thank Malaspina University-College and the Banff Centre for the Arts Writing Studio for the time and place to complete and revise the manuscript.

Robert Pepper-Smith was born in Revelstoke, British Columbia. He now lives on Gabriola Island with his family, where they tend a vineyard. He also teaches part time at Malaspina University-College. *The Wheel Keeper* is his first novel.